CYCLONE

David Penn

A catalogue record for this book is available from the British library

Printed in the United Kingdom

ISBN 978-0-9564941-3-9

Printed by Bonker Books

For the preservation of world wildlife

Synopsis

Cyclone, the story of how nature transformed the lives of three generations, from the green fields of Hampshire, to the harsh, and unforgiving Northern Territory of Australia, unexpected great wealth, the fear and anxiety of kidnap, by Malayan pirates in the strait of Malacca. A page turning adventure story interspersed with the factual devastation of Darwin in 1974.

A tale of lust, luck and excitement, change, choice and achievement.

Dedications

I would like to dedicate this book to my two Grandsons, Bradley and Blake.

Contents

CYCLONE

The Early Days 1957

Chapter 1

COINCIDENTAL

Cedric was delighted, spinning along the country roads on his new Triumph Bonneville. He had just taken delivery and was trying it out, 650 cc. of power, the first of the 5 speed transmission models. He grinned like a child at Christmas.

It was a beautiful June morning, a rare summer's day, the trees and hedgerows shimmered in their fresh green summer foliage and although he could hear nothing with the wind rushing past his ears, he was sure the birds were in full song.

The road curved gently to his right where it widened to accept a branch road on the left. Suddenly it seemed that out of nowhere a silver sports car appeared on his left and cut him up as it swung wide. Cedric stamped on his brakes, and the bike slid wildly and the front wheel and handlebars, and most of Cedric as well, finished up enveloped by the thick undergrowth.

Shocked, he glared across at the driver of the car and managed to extricate himself and the bike and stand it on the road. He inspected the Triumph closely. There appeared to be no damage apart from some wild flowers stuck impudently in the spokes.

"Are you hurt?" The girl called.

"You could have bloody killed me!" retorted Cedric, gearing himself to vent his spleen on the girl, "You were driving too fast and on the wrong side of the road."

"These roads are too narrow for there to be a right or wrong side," she said mildly.

Cedric looked at her open mouthed, he had never heard such female logic in his life. He couldn't help grinning, "Are you from Essex by any chance?"

"No why?"

Having gathered himself he started to see the girl in a different light. She was lovely, fine boned features, long blonde hair doing its best to escape from a colourful head scarf knotted under her chin. It was mainly her eyes which entranced him a deep azure blue, almond shaped and twinkling at him.

"Anyway, no harm done, I must go, I'm in a hurry."

"So I noticed, "Said Cedric dryly. "Before you go any further on your destructive journey, do you know where Hadleigh Manor is? It is around here somewhere."

"I should do, I live there. Why?"

"I have an appointment with Sir. Jonathan Hadleigh."

"Oh, that's daddy," She looked at Cedric, with a new interest. Not a bad looking guy she thought, tall, bit rugged well built. She was secretly pleased to think she might see more of him. "Better follow me then," she called out and drove away.

Hurriedly, Cedric kick-started his bike and raced after her before she disappeared over the skyline.

Some half a mile further on he saw her tail light flash as the car turned into a drive, almost hidden in the lush forest. Ahead there were two large cast iron gates slowly opening. Almost before they were open wide enough the car spurted through. Cedric shook his head. Glad I'm behind her he thought.

The Drive was wide with lush lawn on either side, the extreme edges enclosed by carefully clipped and shaped hedges nine feet high. After a few hundred yards the drive opened into a huge inverted banjo in the centre of which was a magnificent water feature.

"Looks like Venus," thought Cedric. Sparkling water cascaded from an urn perched on her shoulder.

He drove alongside the car as the girl slid languorously out. Cedric caught an intoxicating glimpse of two very shapely calves. She looked back and caught him. She grinned wickedly. Cedric felt colour flood his cheeks.

"Come on then. Come and meet daddy."

The House was huge, imposing with two colonnades dominating the main door. Cedric climbed the steps and followed the girl into a large square foyer, paintings decorated the walls, and the whole area was lit by a massive chandelier. At this time of day sunlight streamed from skylights set high in an atrium. Two Chesterfield settees graced the foyer. Cedric's trained eye saw them as being 19th Century originals, with the influence of Robert Adam's. The whole place was sheer quality without being flamboyant. Ahead was a huge double staircase up which the girl scampered, lifting her white linen skirt above her ankles.

"Someone to see you daddy," she called as a tall, and imposing man walked along the balcony leading to the rooms above.

"So I see. How are you darling?" He bent and kissed her cheek.

"You must be Mr. Weston?" He offered his hand which Cedric, shook, "I am Jonathan Hadleigh and this is my daughter Janine." He turned and smiled at her.

"We've already met." Janine smiled.

"Almost forcibly," said Cedric. Janine stuck her tongue out.

Hadleigh looked puzzled. "Will you organize some coffee Janine, or perhaps you would like something stronger?" He raised an eyebrow.

"No thanks, bit early for me." smiled Cedric.

Chapter 2

RESTORATION

Jonathan Hadleigh was an impressive man, tall with a military bearing and a ready smile his hair was thick and neatly trimmed, wide eyes that were grey and alive. He exuded confidence and breeding.

The room was massive, not a library…not as libraries go thought Cedric, the ceilings were high and elaborately decorated with intricate designs, the walls where they were not covered with free standing bookcases each of which was filled with books of all descriptions, were fabulously covered with a material which, Cedric could not place. They appeared to be individual squares expertly lined up and decorated with the most beautiful scenes and figures which would put Leonardo de Vinci, to shame. The elaborate fireplace formed the focal point and was obviously the original from 400 years ago at least. Cedric gazed in wonder he had never seen anything so beautiful, but the overall grandeur was marred by the bookcases which were as much a part of such historical magnificence as a commode in a restaurant.

"Hadleigh, not what you would expect I think?"

Cedric shook his head.

"Let me explain," said Hadleigh, gesturing for, Cedric to sit in another of the Chesterfields masterpieces. "This room, was originally some 490 years ago the main dining, and relaxation room. The walls are covered with tanned goat skins, each panel a complete skin. The decoration is not only colourful but embossed into skin itself. A unique and expert achievement. The bookcases are really a temporary measure to give storage to the books, many of which are first editions. Remove them, and the whole room will take your breath away. What I want is for the whole room to be panelled in a way that reflects the conventional appearance of a library and covers the original walls, including the fireplace without, and this is very important in any way damaging the original decoration. I understand that this could well be within your capabilities as you are a successful cabinet maker with a history of such expertise dating back to your father, who, I understand panelled a library in Penshurst Place, Viscount de Lisle's, home at the time?"

Cedric smiled, "You have certainly done your homework Sir. but why, why would you wish to cover such magnificence with timber, however exotic that timber may be?"

A sadness flicked across Hadleigh's features. "This room no longer enjoys the dinner parties and convivial evenings it once did. Financially that is a thing of the past, but inevitably the leeches from the Inland Revenue will descend upon the house when I die, and assess it for death duties. I pay £19.6d in the pound on my income so I'm damned if they are going to get any more when I die." He walked across to the fireplace and stroked the smooth stonework.

"The quality and history and the provenance of this room alone, would result in the final figure being 50% higher than the rest of the house. Because of this, a beautiful home will be lost to posterity for all time. I am not a very rich man; I am wealthy but have no heir except, Janine. I would never rest if I left unreachable debts on her shoulders. Does that make sense Cedric?"

"It will be a hugely expensive undertaking," Cedric said thoughtfully. "The timber would need to be the best quality to ensure authenticity, the security of the bookshelves is paramount, and as you say must not violate the walls. But it can be done, it will take some time. I have some pretty skilled people."

"Good, that's that then. The cost is immaterial balanced the ultimate gain."

At that moment, Janine came into the room laden with a tray containing a coffee percolator, cups and saucers, and a plate full of cakes and pastries. She put them on the table and handed tea plates and serviettes around. Having poured the coffee and added cream, she sat herself down.

"Not interfering am I? Time you had a break." She bit into a big chocolate eclair'e.

"Incorrigible," said Hadleigh kindly, "Mr. Weston is going to undertake some work here which will be a long term thing, so I suggest a room is prepared for him should he wish to stay over, and of course, he will eat with us. That will include dinner tonight if you wish Mr. Weston.... unless you have a wife waiting?"

Cedric smiled. "No, no wife."

Janine smiled to herself.

Chapter 3

CONTENT

The next morning, Cedric was just about to mount his motor bike when, Janine dressed in riding gear, and a colourful scarf around her neck called across. "Where are you off to then?"

"Have to go to arrange things with my business and get things moving," he said and then after a moment or two hesitation. "Want to come?"

"Love to." She ran across and jumped on the pillion. "Where are we off to?"

"Salisbury," Cedric kick started the bike into life. "Hold on, away we go."

He wasn't sure why he had invited Janine, but happy that he had, she was a real looker. Cedric was secretly a bit worried, he had told, Hadleigh that he had a good team which was true, but it wasn't a large team. Although he hadn't said as much, he was worried about the ongoing success of his Salisbury business. He would need a lot of help with the project at Hadleigh Hall which would mean neglecting his commitment to customers who were his lifeline. He mentally shrugged, probably worrying about very little; he wasn't going to let Hadleigh Hall go. No expense spared, Jonathan had said and, Cedric had an advance cheque for £1,000 in his pocket. He settled down for the ride. It was a beautiful sunny day and he had a beautiful package on the pillion. Janine squealed with excitement as they leaned into corners and hugged him tightly. He felt her firm breasts squeezing into his back and the feel of her thighs across his hips. He felt excited, and that wasn't only the thrumming of the machine and he was sorry when they arrived in Salisbury, but at least there was the ride back to look forward to. The spire of the magnificent Cathedral stretched upward 223 feet into a cloudless sky, giving directions to all pilgrims for many miles. After turning through a couple of side streets they arrived at, Cedric's home, and business. A large sign above the double fronted building read...

WESTON & COY

Quality Cabinet Makers

Bespoke Furniture Mfrs.

The two large plate glass windows were shadowed as was the door between them. The door bell pinged as they entered and a huge man came into the office from the back. He was at least 6 ft. 2ins weighing around 250 lbs, dressed in brown overalls he ducked under the door jamb. A big grin smothered his ruddy face and extended to his eyes which were merry, and deep brown. His hair was all awry and flecked with sawdust.

"Ceddy," he stuck out a hand as big as a tea plate. They shook hands. Cedric glanced at, Janine who giggled.

"Ceddy?" she mimed. Cedric coloured up and frowned to hide his embarrassment.

"This is Tim, known as Tiny Tim. He's my right arm, so as to speak."

Janine stuck out her hand which disappeared into four sausage like fingers. "Pleased to meet you." He said with a broad West Country accent, "Nice to see a bit of glamour... ugly lot we are."

"Janine laughed, "I wouldn't say that."

"You've not seen the others yet."

"Look," said Janine, to Cedric, "You'll have a lot to talk about, I'll go and do a bit of shopping… see you in a couple of hours."

"Well don't get lost. Salisbury can be a bit difficult to find your way about."

Janine tapped her nose and smiled, "I've spent more of Daddy's money here than he knows about. I know all the expensive shops. See you later." She waved and was gone, leaving a swirl of Chanel as she went…

Tim, gave, Cedric a knowing look, "what you been up to you sly dog you?"

"Bollocks," said Cedric, "come on through, there's a lot to talk about."

Cedric outlined the project to Tim, doing his best to describe the walls in all their glory, he quoted the measurements of the room roughly, there would need to be a much more accurate plan, before anything could be started.

"Do you realize," said, Tim wide eyed, "how much timber this involves, with the quality needed, it represents a bloody rain forest and the cost will be horrendous and that is just the panelling."

"Apparently cost is unimportant." Shrugged Cedric. "The biggest problem is getting the right sort of timber, and not having to wait months for delivery."

Tim and the two most experienced apprentices arrived at

Hadleigh Hall the next morning in order to see for themselves the task ahead. Initially the main objective was to plan, and order the materials which fell to, Tim and Cedric. The two lads returned to Salisbury with strict instructions to look after matters there and to refer to, Cedric with anything out of the ordinary. Cedric spent hours on the phone, locating possible suppliers, none of whom would promise delivery dates, but said they would do their best. The days went by with, Tim, and Cedric, packing the mass of books carefully into boxes, ensuring they were in correct order and were protected. It was hard work but they were looked after by, Janine, who was intrigued with the whole thing and supplied coffee and tea all day, spending as much time near, Cedric as was possible, without making it obvious. To her disappointment the trips to Salisbury, which were quite frequent meant she was left behind as, Tim hooked his ample self on the pillion of the Triumph.

Chapter 4

TRULY

Tim remained in Salisbury whilst, Cedric became almost part of the family at Hadleigh Hall. He felt self-conscious, but needed to be there when the materials arrived. This delighted, Janine, who took it upon herself to take over his spare time. This gradually turned into trips in her car, picnics in the countryside and walks across the downs. This grew into a close, and affectionate relationship culminating in, Cedric, whose feelings towards, Janine, were constantly bubbling over. He one day grabbed her by the shoulders kissing her forcibly, and passionately. This was right in the middle of a public right of way with other couples in the vicinity.

Gasping, Janine pulled back, "I am so sorry," spluttered Cedric, red faced and ashamed. "I don't know what came over me… unforgivable!"

Janine grinned, "About bloody time you big Ape!" She flung her arms around his neck and kissed him back.

Two middle aged ladies in plaid skirts and walking shoes glared at them. "Such an exhibition!" One said haughtily. Janine stuck her tongue out.

Laughing, Janine, and Cedric, wrapped their arms around each other and ran like two school kids along the path and across the field to the river bank. Puffing, they collapsed on the grass still hugging each other.

"What did you mean about bloody time?" Asked Cedric.

"I have wanted you to kiss me for weeks," she smiled "couldn't kiss you first... just not done these days as those two old biddies pointed out... had to wait for you, and God knows it took long enough."

"Sorry."

"Well make up for it now."

They did just that, holding each other and kissing every few minutes. The nearness of, Janine, warm and supple, her body stirred Cedric. He wanted this woman very badly, wanted her for his own, but he knew that could never be. They were in different classes of Society, which would never work in the class distinction of today. He wanted to make love to her, and he could tell that she felt the same, but there were rules. Once that took place there would be no going back for her, so far as he was concerned that wouldn't matter but her reputation would be shot and preclude her from marrying into the social set that would ensure a lavish life style, the sort of life she was used to. He could never provide that.

A deep sigh escaped, Cedric, Janine, sat up and looked at him. "What?" she said," What's wrong....is it me?"

"Yes it is you. I love you Janine, I love you very much, I will always love you, but it can't be, it would never work and you wouldn't be happy."

Janine' eyes flashed and her lips thinned and set hard.

"Really, you honestly take the cake, bloody clairvoyant are you, can see into the future, you don't give a damn how I feel, the fact that I've loved you ever since you appeared on the scene doesn't count. Tell me, Oh Wise One, why won't whatever it is, work, Tell me that? You love me?"

"Of course I do, I think you are the most wonderful person I've ever met… but forgive me, any chance we have together won't work."

"So you say." She got up and walked away turning her back on Cedric.

Distraught Cedric got up and went to her, he put his hands on her shoulders, but she shrugged them off. She was crying, tears filled her eyes and trickled down her cheeks. He took her in his arms and she sobbed into his shoulder.

"What I meant was, that the life I offered would be so different to the life you now have…. I am unable to compete with others who can provide so much more than I can."

"Do you mean that I am doomed to marry some chinless wonder who has no more idea of being a real man, than something out of Madame Tussauds, but has tons of money. I would rather slit my wrists. These gormless idiots who come to Hadleigh Hall with shot guns ready to blast some poor creature out of the sky, who show off their new pair of plus fours and swanky cars, who flaunt in front of me with their suggestive remarks, they make me sick. If I am to marry, I want it to be someone who loves me for being me, who will love me forever, who can give me children that I can love and cherish, who will join me in the ups and downs of life and will grow old with me by his side. I will go anywhere with a man like that, I would be loyal, loving and caring, and happy." She pulled away from Cedric and ran.

"Marry me then!" Shouted Cedric after her.

She stopped. Turned around, and walked slowly back. She sniffed her eyes red and puffy."You are just saying that."

Cedric knelt in front of her and took both her hands in his. "I promise to love you forever to cherish you, and come what may, do all those things to make you the happiest person alive." There was also a tear in his eye.

"You mean it don't you?" she said quietly.

"Yes I really do."

They clung together, both with tears in their eyes, laughing and kissing. After a few moments, Cedric said. "You haven't said yes."

"Oh yes, yes, yes, please………"

Chapter 5

CONFIRMED

"Well," said, Cedric, "that wasn't so difficult, now comes the hard bit. How on earth am I going to get your mother and father to say yes?"

"You leave mum to me, and then I leave dad to mum. All a matter of pecking order you see, dad will never stand a chance, and mum doesn't from me."

"Devious little minx… where do I stand?" Cedric pulled a face.

"Oh, you're a gonna from the start."

Asking Janine's parents turned out to be less traumatic than, Cedric had feared. Dinner that evening was quiet, Janine fidgeting a lot but for once saying very little. Lady Mary was serene as always and showed no signs of any impending trouble. Sir. Jonathan tucked into his food and looked very content. Cedric wondered whether it was up to him to broach the subject and was stimulated by a kick on the ankles from Janine. He glared at her.

"Err, Sir. Jonathan," he began, and immediately forgot what he had intended to say.

"Yes Cedric?"

Plucking up courage plus another kick from, Janine, he tried again.

" Janine, and I, are in love."

"Now there's a surprise," smiled Sir. Jonathan, which took the wind out of Cedric's sails again.

Lady Mary laughed, "John don't make it hard for Cedric, he wants to marry Janine, and it seems, Janine is dead keen to marry him, as you well know… so don't tease."

Sir. Jonathan smiled at Cedric. "We do know through the grapevine known as our daughter, and to put your mind at rest we, Mary, and I, are in full agreement…subject to certain conditions. I have had the opportunity to watch you as you worked on our project. You are a hardworking and sincere man. I feel you will make a good husband for Janine, but there *are* certain limitations, which may, or may not, present themselves. For a start on, Janine's next birthday she will become a very rich woman, as the result of a Trust fund set up years ago. If I had any suspicion that this fact had any influence on your wish to marry…" Sir. Jonathan held up his hand and silenced what was to be an indignant outburst from Cedric. "I would have to reconsider," he continued, "but I do not have any misgivings in that area."

"I am very pleased to hear that." Cedric replied crossly, "so far as that is concerned any money, Janine has, or will have, is her affair and not mine. I feel affronted to hear that you even considered that unsavoury aspect of my feelings. I will do my utmost to provide our marriage with a happy foundation which is up to me."

"I have no doubt that you will succeed Cedric," replied Sir. John, "Forgive me for even broaching the subject; I did not intend any offence. There have been many suitors after, Janine as you might imagine, most of them with pound signs behind the eyes. I have disliked almost all of them, one in particular."

"That was Claude," piped up Janine, "ginger haired twit, I use to call him, 'In and Away,' all he wanted was to get into my knickers and away with my cheque book."

"Janine!" Lady Mary was shocked, "I will not tolerate that sort of language. Sir. Jonathan covered a grin with his napkin.

"Well it's true," said Janine, grinning at Cedric, "I take no prisoners."

"I think Cedric," said Sir. Jonathan, "it is time we disappeared into the nice new library and discussed the benefits of a large brandy. These two will now start planning everything from wedding dresses to babies."

That indeed was the case and the wedding formed part of everyday life. Cedric was consulted now and again and he found it difficult to get, Janine, on her own for more than a few hours at a time. He was however, determined on one thing. One morning he grabbed, Janine, and without explanation sat her on the pillion, and drove away to Salisbury. They stood outside a leading jewellers in Salisbury. Janine peering through the window, her eyes sparkling like the diamonds and jewels displayed inside it.

"Ooh," she breathed, "look at that one and that, they are all so beautiful!"

Cedric grinned, "Lets' go in."

A tall and graceful woman approached with a warm smile.

"I would guess you are interested in either an engagement ring, or even wedding rings?" she said.

"Is it that obvious?" Laughed Cedric. "You're right."

Janine's finger was measured and a tray of rings displayed on black velvet. One ring took her eye immediately, it was a large diamond with two smaller ones set either side. It glittered at her, asking to be tried on. It fitted perfectly. In typical womanly ways she looked at more of the display but her eyes always went back to the first one.

"It's so lovely, Cedric," she said looking hopefully at him.

"I guess that had better be it then." He asked the price.

When told, it made his eyes blink, he looked at Janine, took a deep breath and pulled out his cheque book. The ring was set in a small attractive box and carefully wrapped.

"Can't I wear it?" Janine put on her sad face.

"Certainly not," said Cedric sternly. "Not until the Party."

"What party?"

"The one your mother is organizing with me. Have to have an engagement party, make it all official and let you show off in front of a lot of people."

"Mum didn't tell me." Janine pulled a face.

"She will, you have to send out invitations, and get a new dress!"

That mollified Janine; she danced out of the shop with good wishes from the assistant.

"See you soon for a wedding ring."

The Party was a great success, Janine, and her mother, organized everything and dozens of people, mainly, Janine's friends from University replied and came. Cedric said he had never seen so many beautiful girls in one place before.

"Make sure you just look." growled Janine.

The ring was formally placed on her finger when everyone had a drink in their hands and, Janine, did the rounds of showing it off.

Sir. John grabbed a bottle of Jack Daniels, he, and Cedric then found a quiet place on the terrace to enjoy the dying rays of the autumn sunshine.

"Whatever do they all talk about?" Said Sir John while listening to the hubbub in the lounge. "They never seem to run out of chat." He poured two sizeable drinks and passed one to Cedric. "I am having the Lodge redecorated and refurbished," said Sir. John sipping his whisky. "Fred our now elderly gardener lives there with his wife but the place is getting to be a bit too big for them to cope with. He is going to move to the cottage at the end of the drive that has been vacant for a while since old Percy died. He is delighted. The Lodge will be an ideal place for you, and Janine, to get your feet entrenched into married life and will be yours as long as you wish."

Cedric looked gob-smacked. "John, I don't know what to say? All that you have done for me. I really can't accept all of this. I have been wondering about where we would live after the wedding, but had no idea. It would be perfect of course, but…"

"No buts," smiled Sir John. "I am only too pleased that, Janine loves you, and you her….I am very fond of you, and totally confident that you will be an ideal husband and that you will be very happy together. Not only that, but, Janine is our only child, and we love her dearly, I had feared she might end up with one of those chinless wonders who hover around from time to time like vultures. It should be ready when you come back from the honeymoon."

"Ah. Honeymoon," frowned Cedric, "must do something about that I guess."

"Well," said Sir John, taking a moment to refill their glasses. "I have a friend. Chairman of one of the Merchant Banks I deal with. He owes me a favour. He has a boat, yacht really moored in Ballamadena, Southern Spain. He poodles around the med, from time to time. He has agreed to let you use it on your honeymoon for a week or two, fully crewed... Captain is a Royal Navy retired Captain. Nothing for you to do, everything is laid on and he will sail you wherever you like. All you need to do is lay about and enjoy yourselves. Even got a pool on board...splash pool really. After the wedding you will fly to Malaga, be met, and driven to the Marina, and then in reverse on the way home. That, Mary, and I would like you to accept as our wedding present."

Sir John beamed and took a deep swig of whisky.

Cedric couldn't speak, he felt tears sting his eyes, and he couldn't believe all this was happening.

"John," he stammered. "I don't know what to say."

Sir. John held up his hand, and beckoned one of the temporary waiters. He brandished the now empty bottle...

Chapter 6

MARRIED

The Wedding was arranged six weeks ahead to coincide with Janine's Birthday. That meant, she said, Cedric was less likely to forget their Anniversary! Cedric concentrated on his business over those weeks, attempting to recover from the downturn resulting from his enforced absence. It was difficult. Tim had managed to maintain a happy medium but there had been a loss of orders, mainly from the larger firms who expected a regular supply of the more middle range products. The apprentices were becoming adept and experienced, but it would take time to establish the reputation they had once attained.

The run up to the wedding still took time away from Cedric. Fittings for wedding outfit and although, Lady Mary, and Janine undertook the main needs, there were still a myriad of arrangements to be made. The eve of the day suddenly arrived and almost took Cedric, by surprise. The ceremony was to be held at Hadleigh Hall in the 400 year old Church within the estate. Marquees were erected in the grounds and the place teemed with caterers, florists, hairdressers, photographers and the arrival of guests scheduled to spend the night. They tended to disorganize matters by arriving early and needing to be located. The Bridesmaids needed to be fitted with dresses, previously unable to attend a proper fitting, the twin daughters of Caroline, (Janine's best friend) tended to run riot, and were difficult to tie down for them to have last minute adjustments to their outfits. Tim was to be best man and was nowhere to be seen. Cedric couldn't find Janine. She had disappeared with a bevy of friends, who were trying to make up for the loss of a Hen night. It had been decided that the somewhat riotous goings on at the engagement party would suffice, and, Cedric, found them clustered around a huge oak tree with a number of empty white wine bottles....

"You had better not have a thick head tomorrow." he scolded.

"Imagine having a headache on your wedding night." Shouted one of the girls which set them all giggling....

"Take a packet of aspirins to bed Cedric... that'll fix her."

Cedric grinned and decided he would get no sense out of any of them. He went off to try and contact Tim. He found him on the terrace with Sir. John, doing justice to a large beer.

"They are all mad," smiled Cedric, "under the tree wine tasting, or so they say."

"Have a beer Cedric, and relax," said Sir. John, "You can do nothing more, let the river run."

"Janine says she will promise to love, honour and disobey," said Cedric ruefully, "and I wouldn't put it past her."

John and Tim, laughed. "I think you can bank on that."

The big day dawned and, as Sir. John had said, all went smoothly. Janine looked like a Greek Goddess in a pearl coloured sheer dress with a long train and a figure hugging design. Her hair was down and shimmered in the sunlight, which blessed the October day. There were too many guests to cram into the small church but loudspeakers spread the service and the hymns were sung with gusto inside and out. Before they left, Cedric sought out, Lady Mary. He put his arms around her and kissed on her cheek.

"I just pray, that, Janine will be as wonderful a woman as you, Mary. I am so grateful for everything."

She smiled at him and kissed him back. "Take her, love her and be happy. We all love you Cedric."

Mary's farewell to Janine was a bit more tearful. "Please take this Janine," she said and gave her a wrapped box. Inside was a beautiful gold locket, which when opened had miniature photos of she, and Sir. John. "This locket was my Grandmothers," she said. "My mother gave it to me on my wedding day. I now want you to have it." She fastened it around Janine's neck. "It will remind you always of how much we love you."

"I will never need to be reminded of that," said Janine.

They drove away in Sir. Johns Rolls, en route to the Ramadan Hotel at Heathrow. The Bridal suite was booked for them and the manager had been briefed. Their room was a delight, awash with flowers with a magnum of Champagne in an ice bucket sat on the coffee table. Janine flopped on to the huge bed.

"Wow" she said, "this marriage thing is a bit of alright, I could get used to it."

Cedric just looked at her, "You are beautiful," he said, "and I love you .I always will. You realize this is an important anniversary."

"Of what?" Asked Janine, puzzled.

"When we met?"

"Almost… It is exactly ten months ago when I first wanted to make passionate love to you."

"You poor old thing, to think you have had to wait all this time when you could have done that months ago."

"No... I wasn't willing to buck the system, but there is a pretty hefty backlog to catch up."

"Ooh Can't wait." Chuckled Janine, "but let's crack that bottle of champers first."

Janine came back into the bedroom dressed in a gossamer nightdress which revealed more than it covered. She posed in a provocative stance in the doorway.

"You like?" she whispered.

"Ooh! Yes." Breathed Cedric. His pulse was racing and his breathing was difficult. Janine slid into bed alongside him and snuggled into his arms. His hands explored her slim body and they both became aroused and over eager which resulted in their first lovemaking to be over before they realized. Gasping, Cedric rolled on to his back.

"Well," said Janine, "That wasn't very mind blowing; we need a lot of practice. You can have five minutes off and away we go again. Don't look so unhappy." She kissed, Cedric and grinned at him.

Somewhat mollified, Cedric cuddled her, angry with himself and soon found himself highly aroused again. He cupped his hands around Janine's buttocks and lifted her on top of him. She found herself quivering and aching for him. His hardness pressed into her and he took her breast into his mouth. Janine gasped as he lowered her on to him she cried out. Her body rocked back and forth as she clutched at him drawing his head into her breasts. They climaxed together and collapsed into each-other.

Neither spoke until Janine, said… "Wow! That was the shortest five minutes on record, the future looks bright."

They ordered dinner with room service, unwilling to mix with other diners…

"It will be too bloody obvious." Janine chuckled.

The next morning they caught the flight to Malaga. The Airport was not overlarge and by the time they had collected their luggage, and passed through Customs, they were in the foyer, where friends and relatives of the passengers waved and shouted greetings. Janine walked past a liveried chauffeur holding a white board with, "Mr. and Mrs. Weston clearly marked on it.

"Where are you off to?" Called Cedric laughing, "That's us over there."

"Oh God," she said, "I'd forgotten who I am."

"So soon?"

The journey to Ballamedena took over two hours. The road was narrow, but the time passed quickly. Janine was enthralled with the mixture of fishing villages with potential hotels, and flats, which were growing like mushrooms, and then petered out reverting to the farms and fields of olive trees. At the Marina, which was a mass of weird and wonderful architecture, encompassing yachts and power boats moored higgledy-piggledy, the car took them to a broad jetty. A huge ocean going yacht floated gently on the water, gleaming eye-wateringly white in the brilliant sunshine. The stern was tied up alongside it and, *"MISTRESS OF THE SEAS"* was painted across the stern, bold and proud for all to see. It was a breathtaking sight, brass work gleaming and the decks scrubbed almost as white as the paintwork. A tall and rugged man dressed in uniform stepped across the gangplank on to the jetty holding out his hand.

"You must be the newly–weds?" He smiled, showing firm white teeth, his eyes crinkling with warmth. "Welcome to the Mistress, I am Captain Manisty, Reynard Manisty. I have been ordered to arrange the cruise of your lives, and to spare nothing to ensure your total comfort."

He assisted, Janine, across to the deck and shook Cedric's hand warmly. The Yacht was a *Soraya 46* more like an ocean going Hilton Hotel. There was a Helipad on the forecastle. The accommodation was palatial. More like a luxurious apartment. Everything was upholstered in white leather and the walnut furnishing gleamed. There was an En-suite shower and bathroom, and even a large television mounted on the bulkhead. Janine had never seen anything like it.

"It will take a month to see it all." she said.

A watertight door led on to the quarter deck and ample gilded portholes flooded the whole area with the Spanish sunshine.

"I could get used to this." Janine bounced up and down on the large bed.

"The boat or the bed?"

"Both…"

As promised the honeymoon was a dream, the Mediterranean was kind, and the seas were smooth. Their days were spent swimming and sunbathing, drinking and eating, and making love deep into the night. Janine stood naked in front of the mirror inspecting her tan.

"Coming on nicely, have to do something about the white bits though."

"Don't mess about with those," grinned, Cedric, admiring her. "They are my favourites."

Janine stuck her tongue out. As with all things their time on the boat ended all too soon. They returned home somewhat subdued, but had the new lodge house to move in to. Janine busied herself unpacking a host of wedding presents and putting her stamp on their new home. Cedric eagerly returned to work, anxious about the state of his business. He was concerned with what he found. Two major, regular customers had gone elsewhere, finding that their orders could not be supplied in time, and the smaller outlets were less fruitful than before.

"We are losing money." Tim opened the books and showed Cedric, the bad news. "On top of that Wilson, has declared a wage reduction across the board which has slowed up everyone. We need new outlets, let's hope you can find some pretty soon."

Chapter 7

POSSIBILITIES

Cedric spent long hours developing new contacts with some success, but it was two steps forward, and one back. He could not afford to let his two apprentices go, they were now good craftsmen, and without them, there would be no hope, but the overheads were getting onerous.

At breakfast, Janine, watched, Cedric with concern in her eyes. She took a bite out of a slice of toast. "I've got some news."

"Oh…"

"How would you like to be a father?"

"Yes sure….in the future, some time or other."

"How about next May?"

Cedric thumped his egg and sliced off the top. "We could try then I guess, depends on how things go."

Janine smiled; he is so thick she thought.

"May is about nine months ahead."

The words nine months stirred Cedric's brain. He stopped with a spoon full of egg yolk half way to his mouth and it dribbled down his chin. He looked at Janine quite shocked. "You don't mean…what I think you mean?"

She took another bite of toast. "At last the penny has dropped."

"Are you sure?"

'Saw the Doc yesterday, I'm sure…so is he."

Cedric looked shocked, but then a big grin covered his face and he hugged Janine and kissed her, her eggy chin as well.

'That's marvellous. That's bloody marvellous you clever little thing."

"I would remind you that you had a part to play as well." Janine wiped the egg from her face. "Wait till you're changing nappies."

"Have you told your mum and dad?"

"Not yet, you're the first, apart from the Doc."

"Hope it's a boy." Cedric looked at her expectantly.

'It will either be a boy, or a girl I expect, anyway we wait and see no cheating before."

Needless to say Sir. John, and, Lady Mary, were delighted, their first Grandchild. Sir. John decided the occasion warranted a bottle of Jack Daniels which was duly cracked and dealt with.

There will be no stopping them now." Smiled Sir. John. "Babies for breakfast and dinner."

Janine enjoyed a comfortable pregnancy, she seemed to blossom and suffer no ill effects at all.

"If this is what it does to you we must have half a dozen," grinned Cedric.

Craig was born almost on time; he arrived with very little fuss, and delighted everyone, very few sleepless nights and a voracious appetite. Janine was worried, life as a family had settled into a comfortable routine and there was nothing they wanted for, thanks to the constant care, and attention from her parents. They doted on, Craig, and were always doing as much as they could to make his, and their lives content. There was, however something worrying Cedric. His normal cheerful and up-market attitude was missing and a constant shadow behind his eyes told her something was amiss. It was at breakfast that she tackled him.

"What's wrong Cedric, tell me?" She asked quietly attempting to shovel food into Craig, who insisted on drooling it down his chin.

Cedric looked at her and decided there was nothing to be gained by putting a brave face on, things he knew better than to try and gloss over his concerns.

"It's the business. It is getting nowhere. OK things have picked up but there seems to be no future, not enough anyway for me to be satisfied. I need to make my way in life and provide for you, all of us in fact, in a more constructive way. All we are doing is floating on the generosity of your mum and dad. It won't do."

"They are quite happy about everything, no need to feel under an obligation."

Cedric gave a mirthless laugh. "No need....They provide us with this lovely home, feed us and give us so much. I need to earn my own life; it should be the other way around."

"Why don't you ask daddy to find you a position within his world? He wants to, wants you to do well, It would please him if you asked."

Cedric shook his head, "I couldn't bear working a nine to

five day inside some imposing City building. I would suffocate. I need to use what skills I possess. I am good at what I do, and adaptable, but pen pushing is not my scene."

Janine gave up on a fruitless task of feeding Craig, wiped his face, kissed him and plonked him in the playpen. She rustled through some recent newspapers and unfolded the Daily Telegraph.

"Read that," she said and passed the paper across the table. The Article stood out.

WANTED URGENTLY

Carpenters, cabinet makers, skilled tradesmen in all fields' unlimited opportunities in the building and infrastructure field. Enjoy 340 days of glorious Sunshine, exclusive accommodation and a healthy and happy life under the Australian Sun. For only £10 per head (for adults) children free, make a new, and prosperous life, for you and your family. Apply now to Australia House, The Strand London. Come and talk to us and turn your life around. Telephone...

"Australia?" Cedric looked shocked. "That's a world away, for Gods' sake; I couldn't take you, and Craig, away from your mum and dad."

"Why not?"

"It would break their hearts."

"Well, it wouldn't do any harm to find out would it?"

Cedric looked stunned. "Would you go?"

Janine nodded, "Umm...Love to, big bronzed Surfers, dripping wet pulling me out of the surf...Umm."

"Hussy."

They did go to Australia House. Cedric still in two minds but, Janine, was insistent that there was no commitment at this stage. They waited on seats for an interview with a numbered ticket until called. The walls were covered in posters proclaiming the benefits of the sun sea and sand. The myriad of pastimes afforded by the blue seas, B-B-Q. and views of the Blue Mountains and the Great Barrier Reef. Their interview was conducted by an Australian who was down to earth, encouraging and persuasive.

"Australia is young. Still growing, and will be a world class nation before too long. We can't grow without people, people like you, and your children. The Government is prepared to do all it can to make life as profitable, and enjoyable as is possible. In short there is nothing to lose. There is everything there that you have here, only more of it. We are a bit behind in some things but catching up fast. Most migrants travel by sea but Qantas have just opened up their Kangaroo route. They fly Lockheed Constellations and are in the process of buying Boeing 747s. So far they are offering passage by air to limited numbers, just to fill the seats. You could be lucky."

They provided full details and left with forms to complete and medicals to arrange passports to apply for and a (mass need to do) items. Cedric was quiet on the journey home, not convinced, but not without a sense of excitement of the prospect.

Chapter 8

CHANGES

They said nothing about their trip to Janine's parents, feeling that they should consider what was to be a massive upheaval in all of their lives before making a commitment. They sought no advice from anyone feeling that it was their responsibility, and theirs alone.

"It means selling the business," said Cedric a little ruefully.

"No great loss, its worrying you to death."

"Perhaps Tim would buy it?"

"You could ask."

"Not before we decide."

"Have we?"

"Have we what?"

"Decided?"

Janine looked at Cedric and smiled… "I have, I want to have a go, it's a new country, a new way of life, bit of fun apart from the ups and downs, and ups and downs there will be."

"Bloody hot." muttered Cedric.

"Bloody cold here." grinned Janine.

"Shall we go for it?"

"Let's go tell mum and dad."

The news was a shock to Sir. John, and Lady Mary. The loss of their daughter and their grandson, to a place as far away as was possible was difficult to understand. Sir. John, understood their reasoning and again offered to pull a few strings to find a position for, Cedric, but again conceded that such a move wouldn't satisfy Cedric's need to make his own way.

"We can come home for holidays, or you can come and stay. It's not so far these days; the world is shrinking with the increasing air traffic."

"Will you be able to cope with what is a pretty rough way of life?" Sir. John looked lovingly at Janine, decided that she could and shrugged. "Well then, we had better do all we can to help Mary." He looked towards his wife.

She smiled through damp eyes." I suppose so; you've obviously made up your minds. Anyway it won't be for months yet, there are medicals, paper work, packing and shopping." Her eyes lit up.

It was months, which soon went by, and having carried out all the instructions, they received confirmation of their flight on 1st April.

"Charming," snorted Janine, "Get there, and find they've pulled an April fool's joke!"

Cedric had told, Tim, of their plans and he was delighted, very willing to buy the business and managed to raise a mortgage and renew the lease. An added benefit was the accommodation above the workshop previously used by, Cedric which could now be rented out. Rental accommodation in Salisbury was at a premium. He felt certain he could make a good business again. The flight was long and tiring, Craig was bored, and fractious, and sleep was almost impossible. They flew in a Lockheed Constellation, but ultimately they touched down at Darwin Airport.

Chapter 9

BRETT

"Why Darwin?" asked Janine.

"Luck of the draw." Cedric looked around, there seemed to be little to see. They were subject to a rigorous customs inspection which seemed intent on finding a problem, rather than extending a welcoming attitude. Their passports were taken from them which *was* a bit worrying.

"You get them back after two years," the customs officer growled, "If you want them any earlier it will cost you the equivalent of the subsidized money used to bring you out here, unless there is a genuine emergency when you may be given a temporary one."

Janine pulled a face but said nothing. Having no-one to meet them, Cedric managed to find a taxi driver who took them to about the only really decent Hotel in Darwin. It turned out to be inexpensive, and comfortable and they settled in feeling quite lost. The next day, Cedric, went to the immigration authorities and was interviewed by a burly official who looked bored with life.

"What d'yer want mate?" he asked.

Cedric pushed his documents across the counter. "I believe there are jobs waiting to be filled, who should I see about that?"

"What jobs?"

"As advertised in the UK."

The official laughed. "This ain't the Labour Exchange, any job you want you have to find for yerself. No one here is going to hold yer hand. You want work, get out there and find it like all Aussies do. Can't help you with that."

"But…"

"Next." Looking past him the official called out.

Cedric decided not to pursue the matter and, collecting his papers he walked out, somewhat disenchanted. Deciding to do what was said he walked into the local area and decided to have a beer before doing anything else. Perhaps someone on the pub would help him. He found what appeared to be a pub, albeit from the outside it didn't look too inviting. Inside was exactly as the outside looked. The walls were covered in what had, at one time, been white but now were a dingy yellow, stained with tobacco smoke, the bar stretched along the full length of the room and was a veneer covered surface pitted with wear and tear and cigarette burns. The Barman, wearing shorts, and a stained singlet looked as though the boxing ring would be a more suitable place for him, and gave no sign of having seen Cedric, even though he was perched on a stool in front of him. A few feet away, a large brawny man slouched across the bar, his arms were huge and almost all the skin surface tattooed with fading images. He was drunk, a stained hat tipped on the back of his head which was as round as a cannonball. Sensing Cedric, he turned and rested his elbows on the bar. Cedric ignored him and managed to connect with the barman.

"A beer please."

"Midi or schooner?"

Cedric wasn't sure. "A schooner I suppose."

"You a Pom?"

'I'm English…Yes."

The barman poured beer and slouched away. Tattoo, however, turned his attention to Cedric.

"Another bloody 'Pom the place is full of em. Come out here taking jobs away from the Aussies. Lording it around the place cos they can't make it in their own bloody Country."

His attitude was very belligerent and threatening, Cedric, decided to ignore him. Easing himself away from the Bar, Tattoo turned.

"Don't you ignore me you bastard," he snarled, staggering as he tried to move along the bar, he belched and went to confront Cedric, when suddenly there was a crack like a pistol shot from behind him. Startled, he turned and was confronted by a tall and lean man, dressed in jeans, highly polished boots, a check shirt, and a hat worn rakishly on his head. His hair was blondee and long to shoulder length. He had smacked a riding crop on the bar.

"That is no way to speak to my friend," the stranger said, "you will apologies immediately, you uncouth slob."

Tattoo looked shocked. "Another bloody Pom, the place is crawling with em, who the fuck do you think you're talking to?"

He straightened up, his face flushed, and flexed his huge arms and turned back to face a new target. The stranger stood firm. Tattoo swung a punch and then staggered as his target swayed away from the fist that, had it landed, it would have ended the confrontation there and then. Cedric was shocked, he had never experienced this sort of behaviour and was then even more startled to see the strangers hand, fingers extended stab violently into Tattoos throat. There was an audible crunch as the hyoid bone broke and Tattoo doubled over clutching his neck, gasping for breath. As he bent forward he was struck full in the face with a muscular knee which knocked him backwards, collapsing on the floor with a broken nose and two split lips. The stranger turned his back and calmly addressed the barman.

"Would you please pour two of your best beers and bring them to the table over there, by the window."

The barman was shocked. He had never waited upon anybody in all his life and he wasn't ready to do so now. The look in the strangers' eyes, however, made him think again and he glowered, but went to pour the beer. Taking Cedric, by the arm the new arrival guided him to the table. Cedric was speechless and sat down heavily staring at what was, apparently, his new friend. The man grinned at him.

"Carrington, Brett, Carrington, pleased to meet you." Still bewildered Cedric, shook the hand offered.

"Weston, Cedric, Weston. My God." he said. "That was a bit brutal."

"Must stand up for the old country, can't have these bastards treating us like crap. I take it you are English?"

"Oh yes, not been here long though, only arrived two days ago."

"What are you doing in this Hell hole?"

"Mistake really, I was looking for somewhere to start a business."

Carrington glanced over at Tattoo who was still trying to breathe. Two of his mates had dragged him on to a chair and were trying to stem the blood dripping from his squashed nose. They gave Carrington, some venomous looks but posed no threat. The other customers ignored it all. The barman banged two beers on the table and slouched off.

"What sort of business for Christ's sake!" Carrington chuckled, "This is about the most unlikely part of Darwin to survive, let alone start a business."

"I'm a cabinet maker and a skilled carpenter, make furniture, replica stuff, Chesterfield settees, chairs and tables from a past age."

"You're joking." Carrington's expression annoyed Cedric.

"Very reputable stuff, commands a lot of money," he sniffed.

" You've got Buckley's chance. An orange box with four legs does as a table, put a back on it and you've got a chair, and as for a settee, well I guess only very few know what it is. Maybe there would be a market on the north side in Sydney, where the money is, but Darwin, no chance. What makes you think you can make a go of it?"

"Australia House, they advertised for cabinet makers and based on that we came over, promised me a job, but no-one seems to give a damn. I have no idea where to go, or find these jobs they need filling."

Carrington sighed, "There are no jobs up for grabs. It is

up to you to find work; all they'll offer is making pit props at Mount ISA, in the mines. Are you in the Hostel?"

"No, said Cedric, "in a hotel, I've got a wife and a son, didn't want to rough it with them."

Carrington nodded."There's no money in working for someone else mate. This a big Country and it is going to get bigger. They are doing everything to encourage people from all over to come out here. At present there are only 8 million across the whole land, scattered in the main around the coasts. They want 20 million plus. It is going places this land, with it being over 30 times bigger than the U.K. where you have 60 million. With the influx of all these people, they need food to feed them, they need meat above all else, the Army and other Services, need meat. That is where the money is, breeding cattle. To do that you need land, in fact, like everywhere else land is the best investment, who was it who said, 'Buy land 'cos they ain't making no more? Mark Twain I believe. That is why I'm here, I'm after land."

"Are you a farmer?" asked Cedric.

Carrington laughed. "No I'm a gambler a professional gambler, adept at relieving these guys." He waved his hand in an encompassing sweep around the room, "of all the dough they make in the mines."

"Are you hungry?" Brett rubbed his stomach. "I could eat for England."

Cedric nodded.

"Come on then I know the only decent place in this neck of the woods, Italian, serves great cannelloni, not much else but its good."

They left the pub; Carrington threw a pound note on the bar. "That will cover the drinks and the cost of a taxi for that idiot." He gestured towards the still gasping Tattoo.

Outside was a battered Land Rover, very little original paint could be seen and the cover was torn and ragged.

"That's Tinker, short for tincan. She's like a professional whore, not much to look at but happy when she's flat out." He grinned affectionately at it.

With one loud backfire and a revving of gears they drove through the outskirts of the city and pulled up outside a nondescript restaurant, tucked between a Church and an empty shop with boarded up windows.

"Crafty buggers, said Brett. "They've extended the restaurant into the empty shop behind the windows. Saves local rates wait and see."

Sure enough the seating area was extensive, a highly polished bar skirted one side and the tables were covered with bright crisp tablecloths.

"Stop me making a bloody fool of myself. You're a business man. Two heads better than one as they say, give you a chance to see a bit more of this territory?" He looked hopefully at Cedric.

"Why not?" Cedric was pleased with the offer; he was growing quite attached to this guy and was flattered with the compliment.

"Great, I'll pick you up, what Hotel was it you said?"

" The Darwin Plaza."

"How do they conjure up these names?" Brett grinned, "I'll be there at 8am."

Chapter 10

AUSTRALIA

True to his word there was a loud backfire outside the hotel at 8am and Cedric, clambered into the Land Rover.

"Lovely day," he said.

"They always are, going to keep good by the looks of it. Three hundred days of this sort of thing."

At the Land development office they were made welcome by the clerk, a thin, and slightly balding man with spectacles which, to Cedric's annoyance kept sliding slowly down his nose.

"How can I help?"

"Looking for a spread of land, a going concern by choice, not too large, but large enough to build up. Not too remote and a good price." Brett smiled.

"There are one or two spreads." The clerk was pleased; most of the callers these days were after selling. To have a prospective purchaser was a change.

"You have come at an opportune time. The drought has created a problem with some of them. Joachim Dorovic, is about the keenest to sell. Lost his wife a year ago, then his only son was killed. Destroyed him in effect. Why don't you go see him. He keeps changing his mind, not really with it all the time, but he's a shrewd man, came out her some years ago from Europe somewhere."

"How big is his spread?" asked Brett.

"50,000 acres give or take. Not too large by today's standards."

Cedric blinked.

"Let's have a look then, How far is it from here?"

The clerk slid his specs back up his nose and pulled some maps from a draw. He thumbed through them and extracted a map with a series of red lines drawn across. He set that aside and produced a dog-eared map of the Northern Territory. He ran his finger across the map and described the best route.

"About 100 miles, best way, the main highway takes you to quite near his property. Are you going in that?" He glanced at Tinker, through the window and sniffed.

Craig disdained to answer. It took them just under two hours, with Tinker, doing its best to fracture every bone in their bodies. The property was easy to find, being the only sign of life within the last 15 miles. They drew in along a rutted track and entered through a huge solid gate standing alone without fencing either side. A man on horse-back cantered towards them.

"What d' yer want mate?" He wasn't unfriendly which was as well. He looked as though he could handle himself.

"Mr. Dorovic is he about?" called Brett.

"Inside." He jerked his thumb toward the door set into a large timber built house. There was a wide porch surround the house and the whole structure was built on solid stilts, lifting it two feet from the ground. They clambered out of the Land Rover and rubbed stiffened limbs. Before they could knock, the fly screen door opened and a big man emerged, a broken shot gun under his crooked arm. He was an imposing character, a shock of greying hair and a chiselled face sporting an unruly beard. He had a hooked nose and a dark sunburned face. His eyes were deep set and looked at them with unconcealed suspicion.

"Who are you?" he growled. "What is it you want with me?"

Craig stepped forward and held out his hand. "Believe you are thinking of selling your land, Mr. Dorovic. I could be interested in buying, if it is still for sale."

Dorovic looked at them both for a long moment and decided they posed no threat.

"You'd better come in," he said.

They stepped into what was the main room of the house, the fly-screen door slammed behind them. A huge table graced the middle of the room made from the trunks of trees, trimmed and bolted together. It was over 9 feet long and looked as though it had never moved since being set there. Dorovic nodded for them to sit, the chairs were as solid as the table and took an effort to pull clear. Brett took his hat off and shook his long hair loose.

"Hope we haven't interrupted your afternoon?" he said pleasantly.

Dorovic said nothing, obviously having no time for waffle.

"Who told you I was selling?" He asked.

The Land Registry Office in Darwin."

Dorovic nodded. "You are from England. Da?"

Brett nodded, "and you Sir. are from Eastern Europe, I believe."

"Da! From Georgia." His eyes drifted far away. "I want to go back to my country. I hate this place, hate this Country, it has brought me sadness."

"You have done well though," Brett gestured at the room.

"All for nothing, my wife died…Malaria and complications in childbirth. The child died too. My son, a fine man ready to take over this place was killed soon after."

They were silent, there was nothing to say.

"I have nothing left to keep me here." Dorovic went on. "Do you want to see the place?" They stood up and Dorovic, led the way.

It took over an hour to look around; there was a huge water tank with a windmill working a pump. Too brackish to drink, but good enough for other purposes, sunk into a bore 70 feet deep. There were 6 stables all surprisingly well built, clean and whitewashed. One horse stuck his head over the half door and snickered. Dorovic stroked him and produced an apple from a box outside.

"That is Storm my favourite."

Further on, the bunkhouse was also well built, very spacious and in good condition.

"My men all bunk there. They are good men; nearly all have been with me from the start. They are my friends as well as my livelihood, but not the same as a son of course."

There was a large paddock securely fenced in, inside It was ten sturdy cattle and a massive bull. It stood higher than Brett's shoulders and ignored them.

"Murray Greys," said Brett," probably the best cattle ever produced from the marketing point of view, easy to breed too."

Cedric was surprised, Dorovic, too. He looked at Brett with a newfound respect. "You know cattle it seems?"

"Picked up a bit here and there," he grinned, "He's a prime Bull, Champion I imagine."

"Da, he is a champion, very virile, does his job well….The bastard, I hate him. It was he who killed my son. Went berserk, rammed him against the paddock fence and trampled him to death. I would have shot him dead but they stopped me. Too valuable. I would still shoot him given the chance."

Tour over, they returned to the house and, Joachim brought a bottle of Bundaberg Rum from the cupboard and three glasses.

How many cattle do you have?" Cedric asked.

"Fifteen hundred give or take, last time I looked."

"And the price, homestead, cattle, land all in?" Brett held his breath.

Dorovic said nothing but busied himself pouring three generous slugs of Rum. He passed them across the table.

"Before I say price, there are conditions, firstly my men do not lose jobs. They are good men, you would not find better. Second, my contacts…men who take cattle to the docks will still have the business, they charge sensible rates, and they treat cattle properly. Next the bloody bull is a separate price. He is champion bull, he commands a high price. The sale must be legal, and my solicitor will see that it is. All conditions will be included. Price is £50,000 for land, house outbuildings and cattle. That is £1 per acre, very cheap as long as conditions are met. Should be twice that. Not, how you say, negotiable."

He drank his rum in one swallow and looked straight faced at them both.

Outside, Brett looked at Cedric. "It is cheap, for what there is. He is obviously very keen to sell, have to say sweet words to the Bank Manager."

"How much have you got?" Asked Cedric.

"About £20,000."

Cedric said nothing. He wandered across to the paddock; the air was sweet and cooled by a soft southerly breeze. The Horizon was aglow with the sun low in the sky which was a rich azure blue, there was so much sky. He had never seen so much. A Kookaburra laughed in the distance and crows circled above uttering their sad mournful cawing. 'I could be happy here, he thought. The prospect of again building a business and faced with the obvious lack of demand for his talents did nothing to excite him. It would be a good life for Craig, and Janine. Janine how would she react. Would the climate distress her, she was used to horses, but cattle? It would be tough, especially for a girl used to all the better things in life. And John, and Mary, they wouldn't be too keen on hearing that their daughter was rearing cattle. He wandered back to where Brett was studying the house.

"Needs a bit of renovation," he muttered, "Probably

protected from bloody termites though." He kicked one of the stilts supporting the house. It was solid. They climbed into the Land Rover and drove away. It was some time before either of them spoke. Cedric turned to face Brett.

"How would you feel about a partnership?"

Brett looked startled. "You and me?"

"Listen and don't interrupt," said Cedric. "I've got £30,000 savings, with your £20,000 that would pay for the place. It wouldn't be enough though, there are wages to pay, feed to buy, repairs to be done, a hundred and one things. You would still need to borrow from the Bank, say £10,000 or £15,000 as repayments would start almost at once, but the Bank would be more inclined to lend if we bought the place outright. It would depend on Janine, if she agreed, ok, but if she didn't want to know then that would be that. How do you feel about that Brett, fifty-fifty straight down the middle?"

"Do you trust me that much?" Brett said, "You don't even know me, or much about me. I am really impressed by your offer. I would never let you down. Bloody Hell what a guy you are, what happened to the furniture business?"

Cedric smiled, "That's your fault you put me off that for life." They both laughed.

"Let's go and see she, who must be obeyed."

Chapter 11

THE DEAL

Janine had not met, Brett before; she eyed him with undisguised suspicion. A good looking bloke she thought, English, which is a bonus and Cedric seems happy about him, so that satisfied her. She trusted Cedric's instincts.

Brett looked around the apartment. "Pretty reasonable," he said, "Do you have any furniture coming?"

Janine shook her head, "seemed an unnecessary expense, plus the fact that we had no idea where we would finish up. Where have you two been all day? I'll make some tea and you can give me all the news."

Janine listened quietly as Cedric described the Station, how he had taken to the place, the lack of opportunity in his profession, and the possibilities of a good life and a profitable one. The price was not mentioned.

"From producing furniture to producing meat. Bit of a culture shock, just how do you think you will cope, you know nothing about these four legged beasts, nothing about the system, and even less about the Australian way, plus the anti-pom attitude?"

Cedric had a flash memory of Tattoo, gasping.

Brett butted in, "I think I can help there, I've a deal of experience in most things."

Janine's eyes widened, "you, are part of the deal then?" She looked daggers at Cedric. "You hardly know each other's names, let alone anything about each other? You're not usually so naïve and you haven't told me anything very much. Where's the money coming from, and how much will all this cost?"

Cedric felt he was losing ground. He lifted his hands to pacify her seeing the glint of anger in her eyes. He started with his feeling of peace and tranquillity whilst at the Station, the fact that it was well run and the reason Dorovic, had for selling. The fact that Brett was seeking just such an opportunity without any idea that, Cedric would also be interested. Brett had £20,000 which meant him borrowing a very large amount and the prospect of managing on his own would be awesome. They talked some more until Brett said he would have to go and see the Bank Manager.

"Just you hold your horses Mr. Carrington," said Janine." Before we go any further I want to see this wilderness you're proposing to take me to. You can go buy a car Cedric, something that rides like a real car; I'm not going in that!" She nodded to the window which overlooked the parked, Tinker.

"Please call me Brett."

"Certainly Mr. Carrington, when I, let you call me Janine."

At that moment little Craig, toddled into the room. He looked at Brett, with a frown and went to his father.

"This is Craig." said Cedric proudly. He's two, going on twenty two."

Brett stooped down and held out his hand. "Hi fella, you're a lovely lad my name's Brett." Craig ignored his hand and looked Brett straight in the eyes.

"Bwett." he said. They all laughed and Janine, saw a genuine fondness in Brett's eyes. He gently picked the boy up in his arms and, Craig didn't object.

"I'm your dads friend," he said, "and mums too…I hope," he glanced at Janine, who smiled. Anyone, Craig took to was alright by her.

The two men left rather sheepishly. "Jesus, she's some gal that, women usually do as they're told over here," said Brett, "but anyone as beautiful as she is, are guaranteed to get their own way I guess."

Cedric grinned, "she's great, knows her own mind, and takes no prisoners but she's wonderful, just don't make a pass at her you'll never recover."

They went to see a Car dealer Brett knew. He seemed to know a lot of people thought Cedric. They obviously knew each other.

"Need a car," said Brett, "none of your normal shit, good nick, reliable, guaranteed, taxed and ready to go! Full tank as well."

"Don't want a couple of blonde Sheila's in the boot I suppose, you cheeky bastard."

"Only if you insist Wally."

He turned to Cedric, "This is Wally Murphy, the only honest Irishman in the Antipodes."

"Pleased to meet ya," said Wally, "how d'ya come to fall foul of this reprobate?"

"He just sort of appeared."

"Don't play cards with the bastard he'll take the skin off yer back."

"Who's buying the motor then, and if it's you," he nodded at Brett, "you better not think I am taking that in part exchange, my reputation would go straight down the gurgler!" He nodded at Tinker.

"What reputation is that?"

Wally ignored him and beckoned them to follow him.

There were dozens of cars and Ute's, as the Aussie calls an open backed Estate. He opened the doors of a large garage, come workshop, in which there were six, or seven vehicles. At the back was a large Holden Estate.

"Just finished work on this, she's a beauty, bloke couldn't find the repayments. I did him a favour and bought it off him. Poor guy."

"Yeah right," muttered Brett.

They looked it over; it was roomy, clean and undamaged.

"Why the Hell do they build these things with plastic covered seats in this climate?" asked Cedric.

"Easier to clean if someone chucks up after too many beers."

There was no answer to that. Wally started the car and drove it out.

"Take it for a run," he said, "take it easy though it's a four litre engine…goes like shit off a greasy shovel."

Cedric bought it after a lot of good natured insults, Wally even filled the tank.

The following day they drove to see Dorovic again, this time arriving more refreshed and in better time. Dorovic had asked his solicitor to be present; a dour man with a broad Scottish accent, his main point was that the figure of £50,000 was too little for what was included in the package. However Dorovic was insistent that all he wanted was that amount of money, what was more important was the welfare of his men, and the survival of the farmstead. Janine listened intently and then asked, Brett, and Cedric, to show her around. She was impressed, and said so.

"I think I feel much the same as you Cedric," she said "this will be a lovely place to live, a healthy place for Craig, but it needs a lot doing which will cost money. I propose that we form a partnership, £20,000 from each of us which will give us a chunk of dough to use for immediate use, and make it unnecessary for Brett to borrow any money. It would be bad business to start whilst being in debt and have to pay interest."

Cedric started to argue. "What money are you talking of, if it's your trust fund you know how I feel about that."

"It's my money and I am the one who decides what to do with it!" She retorted, "And without me, you two would fail in no time. I know what I am talking about, I had a good teacher, and my dad would have a fit if you two blew whatever you've got for the sake of seeing some common sense. Either you agree to it, or I shan't entertain coming here." Her eyes glinted and Cedric shrugged, he knew she was right.

Chapter 12

LIFE AT LAST

The deal was struck and after cheques changed hands, there was one last suggestion by Brett.

"How would you feel Mr. Dorovic if your prize bull stayed here to service the herd, we would ensure he was looked after and pay you a service charge each time he had his way with the ladies. That way we both score."

Dorovic grinned, "Sounds good to me."

After they left with the assurance the place would be ready as soon as the cheques cleared, Janine looked at Brett. "Not just a pretty face are you? That was a clever stroke."

"We studs have to look after our own." He grinned.

They named it The Double C Cattle Station, and moved in ten days after the signing.

A meeting was called for all hands, which included Ho Chin, a very fat, round faced Chinese cook. When introduced he bowed low to everyone and said.

"I velly good cookie, I have wecipes fwom my gweat gweat gwandfather. You will be velly pleased with me."

His cue, or pigtail wiggled at the back of his head and his moustache sprouted from his upper lip to below his chin. At least it did on one side, on the other it finished abruptly after only a couple of inches. Janine was intrigued.

"Why is your moustache shorter on one side Ho Chin?" She asked politely.

"Set the bloody thing alight didn't he, cooking one of his flambé wecipes," laughed Rick Langton, the main drover. Ho Chin looked ashamed.

"I like it," Janine smiled at him, "it's different."

Ho Chin brightened up. There were 15 station hands, all of whom attended the meeting. The atmosphere was one of suspicion, and distrust. They didn't like change. New ownership usually meant unpleasant interruption to their way of life. Besides these people were Pommies, what the Hell did they know about Australia, or in particular the running a cattle Ranch. Cedric stood up and called for silence.

"First I would like to put you minds at rest; there will be no alteration to the running of the station. Each, and every one is a valued member of the team of whom Joachim Dorovic, speaks very highly. We are looking for your help. We know little, or nothing of this way of life, so we shall depend on you all. We are English, which I know lends itself to some ribald comment from the Aussie, I ask that you judge us for what we are, and not allow any resentment to influence our relationship."

There were some amused glances that passed. "Your rates of pay will remain the same, except," More anxious glances, "there will be a 10 percent increase across the board as from next Monday."

This resulted in a couple of "Good on yer shouts," "and on top of that I intend to introduce a bonus scheme based on profits every three months, In that way everyone will feel part of the business instead of feeling that you work for us. If anything needs doing or improving, please let us know, and any gripes come to me instead of to each other. Finally there will be a B--B-Q. on Saturday to celebrate the launch of what I hope will be a profitable, and enjoyable business. Any Questions…?"

"Yeah, the Drover grinned, "How's yer missus going to cope with riding, we all live on a horse, just wondering if any of us can help?"

The question was loaded with innuendo, with hardly disguised sexual implications.

Janine narrowed her eyes, *"I have* been on a horse before just wondering if you'd like a race, three of you superb horsemen could race me over a mile and a half just to let me get the feel of an animal again." She looked innocently at the drover.

"No worries Missus we can arrange that. I guess you could ride Thumper, he's pretty easy going."

'Thumper…?"

"He's a young Stallion, strong and willing."

There were a few murmurs of concern amongst the men which Janine, caught.

"Great," she said. "How about Saturday? Make it part of the B- B- Q?"

Cedric looked worried, and Brett, looked absolutely terrified, until, Janine winked at them both. Cedric whispered to Brett.

"She's been with horses all her life but don't tell anyone."

Later Janine wandered over to the stables and looked up Thumper. He was a beautiful horse big boned with a deep chest and intelligent eyes. She opened the door and went in carrying a couple of apples. The horse, looked at her suspiciously and snorted. He stomped the ground with a forefoot. Janine stroked him gently and moved in front of him looking into his eyes and breathing slowly into his nostrils. She gave him an apple and talked to him, playing with his ears whilst he chomped the fruit. She moved around him stroking and soothing. Thumper stood quietly turning his head to see where she was. She stayed for half an hour talking to, Thumper and stroking his nose, breathing gently into the flared nostrils. Finally she gave him the other apple and walked out of the stable. Thumper turned and followed her, sticking his head over the half gate, watching where she went. He whickered. Janine smiled and walked away.

....

The day of the B-B-Q arrived and with copious quantities of food and beer, all was set for the celebration. Hanging in the air was the prospect of the race. Janine arrived resplendent in jodhpurs and a coloured shirt which drew some astonished looks from the men. To see a Sheila, in trousers was one thing but in buttock-hugging jodhpurs was something else. She allowed one of the men to saddle Thumper, for her, more out of playing the innocent female than disclosing the fact that she could easily have done it herself. She walked around Thumper, and played with his ears. He half closed his eyes with pleasure. In full view she then vaulted easily from the ground and settled gently into the saddle. She grinned, and gently urged Thumper into a canter around the paddock. The shocked silence spoke volumes.

"Ready then?" She called, "up to the single gum and back, last one scrubs out the Dunny."

Three other hands lined up alongside her. Cedric lifted a handkerchief and with a flourish brought it down. They raced off. The three hands aimed for the gateway out of the paddock but, Janine, steered Thumper to the fence, she leaned forward and stroked his neck.

"Come on baby, come on over." 'Thumper responded well she made sure he was foot sure and at the fence she lifted him up, and over, with 2 feet to spare, back legs tucked under, and forelegs landing securely, he flew ahead of the others. Janine patted him and tickled his ear; the horse whickered and with ears back entered into the race with gusto.

"Look at that bloody horse," Yelled one of the other riders. "Never jumped a fence in his fucking life, only ever jumped a mare."

The three competitors, already ten lengths behind, were completely gob-smacked and shocked. Janine reached the half way point and swung around the huge gum tree flying for home before the others reached the tree.

"Don't forget the Dunny." She shouted.

Thumper thundered into the paddock Janine, hugged his huge head. "You belong to me now," she said and set about drying the perspiration from his gleaming body as the others entered the paddock.

"You took us for a bloody ride Missus," the Drover said ruefully.

"You shouldn't make assumptions." Janine grinned. She

stuck out her hand. "You never know when they come back to bite."

The Drover shook her hand, "You're a bloody fine horsewoman," he said with a smile, "You'll be right."

He turned to face Jeff Baldwin, "Get that Dunny scrubbed Jeff."

The Station worked well, the Bull did his job and the heifers were pregnant, with those who already calved there was soon a small herd ready for shipping and the prices were high. As Brett had forecast there was an urgent need for good quality meat, and the buyers made a point of looking out for cattle from the Double C Station. The bonus scheme worked well, and the hands enjoyed extra money to pour over the bars in Darwin, and some went into the pockets of the willing girls who catered for the other needs. There were rarely any problems, and the three of them generated a respect which made life rich and rewarding. Gradually the reputation of the Double C Station, grew more and more, and the demand for good quality beef ensured a good market price and a constant provision of cattle. Profits enabled, Cedric, and, Brett, to expand the herd and they had to seriously consider buying more land to ensure quality feeding. Craig continued to grow and become more and more involved in the running of the Station. It was hard work, but, Craig thrived, and grew, becoming tough and sunburned.

Chapter 13

CRAIG

Craig was about to ride his 16th birthday present. Confident that it was a larger edition of Minty, his favourite pony, he walked purposefully towards *Caliph*. The horse stood still, apparently disinterested in all around him. There was a tension in its legs, betrayed by a gentle quiver. It looked at Craig, with a suspicious gleam in its eye as, Craig approached it and threw a blanket across its broad back. A pure bred Arab stallion, it stood tall showing off its beautifully chiselled features, arched neck and a magnificent tail high on its rump. It was black, black as wet coal, and the coat shimmered in the sun. The horse was a gift to, Craig, from his father, a combined pre-Christmas and 16th birthday gift. Bred from the Sire, Sultan, owned by Geoff Nixon on a neighbouring station, and with Cedric's own Arab mare, Seraph, It had grown on Geoff's Station to its present size, and was considered to be a prime example of its breed. They had named him, *Caliph*, and it had cost, Cedric and Janine, a lot of money, but a further dig into Janine's trust fund had covered that. Craig who had ridden horses albeit they were ponies, although Craig, would never admit it. Janine would never allow her boy to risk a broken neck falling off a fully grown animal but, was totally confident about his ability to tame this half a ton of horseflesh.

Jarra the adopted member of the family stood quietly by the corral gate. He was an Aborigine, a descendant of the Ngoni Tribe, who landed in Australia 40,000 years before. Built like a stick with the wood scraped off, he was in fact very strong and had proved himself invaluable to Cedric, from the early days of his arrival. Craig had been playing near the outer fence and Janine, concerned as to where he was, saw Jarra, a tall black, half naked figure running toward Craig. She screamed and rushed across to grab, Craig before this savage did. Jarra reached Craig, and swept him up into his arms and in the same movement grabbed what appeared to be a stick. He flicked it like a whip and tucked it under the thong around his waist. Grinning he handed Craig, to his mother.

"Him bad snake…he bite baby, no chance."

Janine was speechless, "You saved his life."

Cedric and Brett, hearing her scream had arrived.

"That's a bloody brown snake, deadly bastard. Little feller would have been brown bread by now." Brett stepped forward and shook the hand of Jarra. "Well done black feller," he said.

From that moment on, Jarra Bulla became part of the family. His aptitude with horses and animals was amazing, and he was offered a job looking after the horses. As Craig grew he became attached to Jarra, and in turn Jarra, cared for him consistently. Craig was taught how to survive in the outback, how to recognize the spoor of a Kangaroo, how to tell how big it was as opposed to a wallaby. He taught Craig, to run when he was six.

"You run like a fat wallaby, you must breathe as you do when you swim. Three steps breathe out, three more you breathe in. keep knees a little bent make them springs."

The septum of his broad nose had an incision to accept a piece of polished kangaroo bone, but the bone was now used for his religious treks into the outback. Janine had said it made her feel sick; his thick curly hair had slivers of silver in it now as did the thin beard which followed his chin line from ear to ear. How old he was no-one knew, least of all Jarra, the passing of time was of no consequence to the Aborigine. He had shrugged off the ribald comments of the station hands and showed no sign of being stung by their racist taunts, until they tired of trying to goad him and left him alone. The one thing an Australian, cannot stand is having no reaction to his bully boy attitude, Janine, grew to trust him implicitly. Craig adored him and went everywhere with him. If ever the cry went up. "Where's Craig?" He was always with Jarra. The only thing the station hands wouldn't have was Jarra, sleeping in the bunkhouse. That didn't bother Jarra, he preferred sleeping, either in the open, or with the horses. He taught Craig how to find water where there was none, how to locate a tree with witchety grubs beneath the bark. How to build a fire safely without risk to the tinder dry bush. There they would eat snake and witchity grubs, Craig, was told never to tell his mother about that! Jarra ate the grubs as they were…Craig preferred to impale them on a stick and watch them sizzle. When he was fourteen he could run with Jarra, in that long loping stride that covered distances seemingly in no time, and not be out of breath. He could bring down a fat Galah, with the boomerang which Jarra, made for him and taught him to throw, and stun a Big Grey Kangaroo, with a throwing stick from 50 yards away.

Jarra would smile and say. "Now you just need bone through nose."

As he reached sixteen Craig, was a match for any athlete. Broad shoulders, long muscled legs, and biceps to make any fully grown man envious, he had a macho bearing and was about to show off. Craig not allowing himself to be disturbed by this animal, swung himself effortlessly across its back. *Caliph* stood quite still, and Craig, grinned at Jarra. Without any warning the horse threw his back legs high in the air, and came down with a thump and reared up. Craig flew backwards and landed in an untidy heap on his backside. Jarra kept a straight face but his eyes danced. Picking himself up and rubbing his rump Craig, glared at the horse.

"You bloody donkey," he roared.

"Language," he turned to see his mother leaning on the fence, blondee hair rustling in the wind below a large Stetson.

"Blow up his nose?" called Jarra.

"What…?"

"Breathe into his nose, and play with his ears."

"You're joking the thing hates me."

"Horses don't hate, only man knows how to hate. Make him your friend and he will love you forever."

"Yeah Right!" Muttered Craig, still believing Jarra, was joshing him but he walked gingerly in front of *Caliph*, and looked at him, putting a severe frown on his face. Two dark eyes looked back at him, was there a twinkle there? He breathed slowly into the wide nostrils and Caliph snorted, right into his face. Craig pursed his lips and tried again, at the same time taking both of Caliphs ears in his hands. To his amazement a dreamy expression came over the horse, the ears tweaked under his hands and it shuffled with obvious enjoyment.

"See," Jarra called, "talk to him, it doesn't matter what you say just make it sound friendly."

"Who's a rotten bugger then." Craig glanced guiltily at his

mother, who was watching and thoroughly enjoying, Craig being set up by a horse. "You chuck me off again and you're off to the glue factory."

"Now walk away, leave him for a minute or two and then give him this." Jarra threw an apple to Craig, who caught it deftly. He walked away, avoiding the back legs as he did so.

Caliph followed him, slowly, right across the paddock. Craig stopped and the horse stopped. He gave *Caliph* the apple. Taking it with his teeth he held it, undecided whether to eat it or not. Then with a crunch it was gone.

"Now what?"

"Try again." laughed Jarra.

This time, *Caliph* stood still as Craig mounted. He leaned forward and tweaked his ears, and gathered up the reins. Two gentle thumps with his heels and Caliph moved forward. Elated, Craig guided him through the gate and into the scrub. *Caliph* picked up its gait and trotted along, apparently at peace with the world until it stopped suddenly and dropped its head. Craig flew forward over *Caliph's* head and landed, once again on his rear. He stayed where he was and glared at the horse that trotted over and nuzzled Craig's neck. It was then that, Craig saw the funny side of the circus. He got to his feet and rubbed his behind.

"Alright....you win."

He grabbed the reins and vaulted on to the saddle with a gasp of pain. He turned towards the paddock and urged, *Caliph* forward gripping tightly with his legs, and holding on to the flowing mane.

"Chuck me off again and half your bloody neck comes with me."

They trotted into the paddock and with a pull on the reins *Caliph* stopped gently as he slid off his back. Jarra threw another apple, which, *Caliph*, took and munched straight away. Janine and Jarra, clapped and Craig, took a bow, pain shooting through his backside. As he hobbled away he noticed with a wry grin that the horse walked behind him.

"Gotcha." He said.

Chapter 14

CYCLONE

You'd better take a look at this Greg." The deputy Meteorological Officer spun round on his wheeled chair and called across to his chief. "Looks a bit ominous but could be bugger all."

Greg Garrison put down his coffee reluctantly. He had been trying all morning to inject some caffeine into his brain. These pre-Christmas parties were all very well, but the next morning they bit back. He stretched his neck and grimaced that had made things worse. He walked across to his Deputy and peered at the screen.

"What!" He hadn't meant to be so sharp.

"That!" Said Bruce, his face registering displeasure at being snapped at.

"You're not the only one who didn't know what time to go home last night! Up there close to Bathurst. The pressure is low across there and the sea surface is above 30 degrees centigrade. Could be a bit unstable. Nothing much at the moment, still 300 km away. Worth watching though."

"I guess so," said Greg, frowning, "nothing to get our jock-straps in a twist about."

Bruce shrugged, "Don't forget, Ada and Emily, though."

"Who the fuck are they?"

"Bloody Cyclones. Ada cost $390 million and Emily, blew

eight seamen away. We didn't take a lot of notice then either, not until it was too late."

"Yeah well keep an eye on the situation, don't want to go off half cocked." Bruce shook his head and then wished he hadn't. He too had imbibed not wisely but too well at the party. He couldn't remember whether he had eaten burgers or snags, or whether he had eaten at all. "No more drinking for a month," he muttered to himself, knowing full well there was as much chance of sticking to that as there was seeing a rainbow at midnight.

The next morning there was a change, the air had become very still and humid and the unstable conditions had intensified and formed a tropical depression which had started to move slowly south west. Moving clockwise, and spiralling high across the brassy sky. It was still 200 km. distant skirting the edge of Bathurst Island.

Greg was worried. "We should report this as a cyclone, but not to panic. It is going to miss Bathhurst and blow itself out over the Timor Sea."

"It's already about 500 km across," Bruce clicked buttons on the machine which showed wind direction and strength. It could miss us but its arse end could do some damage."

"Send all the details to the N D O. Nothing too dramatic otherwise we shall look like a flock of Galahs if the bloody thing peters out."

"What do we call it, apart from the obvious?"

"Hang on," Greg went to a cabinet and fingered through the files, coming up with a red folder. He opened it and thumbed through the pages. "Jesus it's a wonder we've not been blown

away with all these bloody cyclones. The next one is *Tracey.*
Sure to be a Sheila as most of 'em are."

"Wonder why?" grinned Bruce.

"You're not married, otherwise you'd know."

Bruce was not at all easy about the situation, he had seen
too many of these tropical storms turn into a frenzied devil,
plus the fact that they could change direction in a nana second
and catch even the most experienced meteorologist with his
pants down. The land temperature could well feed it to double
the size. On the 23rd of December, Bruce's fears were justified.

"The bitch is swinging 280 degrees towards Point Blaze and
Anson Bay," he called to Greg. "Once it hits land, Christ alone
knows what it will do."

Greg looked at the screen and immediately instructed
the team to come to full alert status. "Send urgent alert to
Darwin…Townsville and Katherine. If this hits the City, God
alone knows what will happen."

"It could change direction again." Bruce didn't sound too
convinced.

"I don't give a shit; I don't want to be on the end of a
witch hunt because we didn't react. Personal message to Major
General Stretton, the DG National Disasters Organization he
can carry the can but at least he will have been told."

The information passed stimulated immediate action, and
arrangements were made to prepare for evacuation. Police
patrolled the streets warning of possible devastation; and
advising as to areas where people could take cover. The traffic
built up with cars and lorries filling the highway south, coaches

were laid on, and Darwin became a hive of panicking people instead of a City dozing in the sun. As Bruce had anticipated the storm hit the coast and writhed into a colossal 600 mile heaving mass of black cloud, resembling a gigantic black and grey blancmange, seemingly only just above the ground. Forked lightning splintered across, and through the cloud and at Blaze Bay, a sea surge drowned the land under 30 feet of raging water. The wind intensified to 150 km per hour and lashed rain horizontally as once again it swung eastward and headed straight for Darwin. At 4 am on December 26th in 1974 *Cyclone Tracy*, ripped into the city of Darwin with a force previously unknown, even in the land of cyclonic violence. Tearing up everything in its path the twister demolished 90 % of the housing, and severely damaged the more robust buildings. Hurling cars and vehicles into the air like leaves in a high wind, it screamed its way searching for the most vulnerable. Communications were lost and power destroyed, electric lines ripped apart, spluttering in torrential rain which flooded roads feet deep, and made emergency services helpless. 20,000 people were made immediately homeless, 44 died, and the hospital was badly damaged. The winds destroyed all commercial aircraft, and the airport was decimated. An R A N Patrol boat sank drowning one crew member and leaving another missing. Water supplies were polluted by broken sewer pipes, giving rise to the fear of infection.

The Minister of Defence Mr. Barnard made the whole resources of the Nations Defence Forces available, and the whole City was declared a disaster area. Darwin faced an unbelievable future, the cost of resurrection running into multi-millions of dollars and the livelihood of thousands in peril. The World Health Authorities were involved and donations of clothing, tents, medical supplies and blankets were desperately sought.

The Hospital was partly demolished, and patients were shifted into marquee's specially erected. Happily the operating theatre was untouched but it was days before power and water could be connected. Those uninjured from Darwin and surrounding stations and townships, converged on the city and worked to help through the days and nights, sifting through the rubble and occasionally locating a victim buried beneath the debris.

Chapter 15

BACKLASH

Jarra stopped and turned his head westward. He, and Craig were riding east across the extent of Cedric's land on one of their forages into the outback. Jarra was worried. The air had turned heavy, and humid, the sky brassy and unnaturally dark. Jarra sniffed, his wide nostrils taking the scent of the air. He frowned.

"What's up?" Craig reined in *Caliph,* and looked quizzically at Jarra.

"Bad, bad wind," Jarra looking more worried than Craig, had ever seen him. "Big storm coming."

Craig looked at the Sky, "summer storm I guess," he said.

Jarra shook his head, "Much worse, come, quickly we must find shelter."

At that moment the first gusts of wind tore at them spewing hard icy rain which felt like mini bullets. The first rolling thunder claps echoed across the land, and lightning forked, lighting the gum trees and giving the whole place an eerie, and ghostly feel. Craig needed no more convincing he spurred Caliph, into a gallop and they fled the rain. The horses whickered with fear and needed no urging.

"Where?" Called Craig, "where can we go?"

The land was desolate with hills and gullies, threatening to fell the horses. Soon the water sloshed around the horses hooves, the land had been so dry for so long it could not absorb the downpour.

"The old mines!" Jarra shouted but his voice was smothered in the wind.

"What?" called Craig. Jarra just waved Craig on.

After ten minutes the landscape changed and became more mountainous, trees now bending in the ferocious wind, branches snapped off and flying in all directions the water getting deeper by the minute. Ahead, although difficult to see through the downpour, a dark earthen mouth appeared, not more than ten feet high, but wide and threatening. Jarra rode straight at it and disappeared into what now became a tunnel carved into the earth and rock. *Caliph* shied and whinnied with fright but Craig, coaxed him and they followed Jarra. Inside, Craig, ducked to avoid slamming his head on some rotting timber above. Suddenly the wind ceased and the rain stopped, the oppressive silence a shock after the outside cacophony. The noise took on a new timbre the shrieking wind and thunderous rain echoed into the tunnel and took on an even more threatening sound than ever.

"Where the Hell is this?" Craig peered around in the darkness which was lit by frequent flashes of lightning. Jarra was stroking his horse and soothing its trembling.

"These are...or were....the gold mines from years ago. Gold was found by one, lone, prospector...Not much, but enough to stir the greed of others. He took his finds to the assayer in Katherine...the word soon got around and he was followed back to his site. He had not staked a claim, nor registered the place. They murdered and robbed him, and soon there were dozens of seekers of the yellow metal swarming over the hills and river. It was not long, a year or two, for the whole place to be riddled with tunnels and excavations and for it to be obvious that there was not enough gold to fill a billy can. Now it has been deserted a long time. Nothing but broken shovels picks and hearts. White men are greedy and vicious."

"How did you find this place?" asked Craig. Jarra grinned a wide grin...

"I find everywhere, sometime, my father brought me here to see how foolish white men waste their lives."

Suddenly the place became silent. The rain had stopped, the wind died and the sudden silence, was almost as terrifying as the uproar before.

"There it is over." smiled Craig.

Jarra smiled and shook his head. "Just the eye, we are in the middle of the tornado, all will be hell let loose again, soon when the outer rim comes."

He squatted down and closed his eyes. As Jarra predicted the storm returned but without the same intensity, swinging towards Arnhem land and the Arafura Sea where it blew itself out. Craig and Jarra, were not aware that they had experienced only the outer edge of the tornado. Darwin had taken the full force of *Tracy*. She struck the semi prepared City early on Christmas Day with a viciousness, and brutality, almost unequalled in the history of Australia's worst cyclones. The outer periphery of the tornado struck Craig, and Jarra. Hailstones as big as golf balls thundered down coating the ground with ice, and more and more torrential rain poured horizontally. Almost ready to ride out of the cavernous entrance to the mine they backed further in. Suddenly as though a switch had been thrown the noise stopped, the downpour abated to heavy rain, and an eerie silence ensued.

"That should be it now," said Jarra, peering through the rain into the clearing sky. "We had better make tracks to see how the Ranch has fared."

As they cautiously made their way out of the mouth of the mine there came a deep ominous rumble from deep in the earth, they stopped and tried to locate the cause. It grew louder and the ground began to tremble. The horses whickered and panicked bolting out of the entrance.

"It's the mine," shouted Jarra. "It's collapsing, falling in on itself. Get the Hell out of here."

It wasn't necessary to goad the animals they galloped out in a frenzy both riders clinging on for dear life. The ground was heavy with thick mud and their hooves sank inches deep, slowing them up. The roar of the collapse grew in intensity looking back, Craig saw an amazing sight. The whole side of the mountain was sliding on to the mine area; a huge crater had opened into which the mountain, was tumbling the screeching of snapping timber and twisting metal. The noise was horrendous, and the horses struggled to free their hooves from the clinging mud. At last they managed to clear the sucking mud and found firmer ground, the horses relaxed, and though still scared they made their way homeward.

Caliph was hobbling favouring his right foreleg. "*Caliph* has gone lame," called Craig, as he slid off the horses back. He lifted the lame foreleg and wiped the mud away from the hoof. Stuck in the frog was a large pebble of stone. It was dry and caught the daylight with a glitter. "Pretty thing," muttered, Craig, and stuffed into his trouser pocket. There seemed to be no further problem but he cleaned the hoof out and checked on the other three hooves. All seemed well and Caliph, snorted and was eager to get going again. They galloped furiously toward the Ranch, frightened of what they may find.

"If it hit Darwin it may have skirted the Ranch." said Jarra.

"Let's hope so," Craig muttered grimly, urging *Caliph*. The horse snorted.

They arrived back to see, Cedric, and Janine with half a dozen Ranch hands standing outside the house which, thankfully was intact. They waved and received some hectic waving back.

"Where the Hell have you been?" Asked Brett, "we've been worried to death."

"Almost buried under a bloody mountain." grinned Craig. "How about you lot?"

"All sheltered under the house bar, one of the guys got blown off his horse and broke his arm, no-one else was hurt."

"*Caliph* picked up a stone in his frog mum," said Craig, "this one." He pulled the stone out of his pocket.

Janine looked at it, "Pretty, I'll have a look at *Caliph*, see if there is any damage."

She put the stone on the mantelpiece and went to find the horse. There was quite a bit of superficial damage to the outbuildings but nothing that couldn't be fixed. Ho Chin, fixed one of his special dinners and life again settled down. The devastation of Darwin had an effect on the Ranch, the port was disorganized and loading cattle was somewhat chaotic, but gradually some order was being restored. Water and power were the big problems.

Chapter 16

ENDURANCE

Later Cedric called Craig into his study. "Sit down Son," he said, "I have something to tell you."

Puzzled, Craig sat down; he could see his father was serious and wondered what he had done wrong.

Cedric lit his pipe, "This Ranch is doing OK and beginning to reach the higher levels of productivity. In some ways it is getting to be too small to allow expansion, and unless we do expand we are going to be overtaken by the big boys."

Craig nodded, wondering what was coming. He could never have guessed.

"We, your mother, and I." Cedric went on, "Have decided to expand your mind, give you an education over, and beyond, that, with this home schooling by radio can give you. You are a very bright lad and you have absorbed a lot of knowledge and ability but you are missing out on the big wide world outside Australia." Cedric lifted his hand to stop Craig, objecting as he saw he was. "With the aid of your Grandfather, and your Aunt Maud…"

"Who the Hell is she?" Interjected Craig, getting a bit worried as to where all this was leading.

"My maiden sister," said, Cedric lives in Winchester. A lovely lady, only ever seen you once when you were first born."

Your Grandfather, being who he is, has managed to pull a

few strings and secured a place for you at Bramington Public School, in Winchester." Craig was too shocked to say anything.

It is very rare that any boy of 16 years of age is admitted, mostly they start at Bramington at 11 but an exception has been made for you to spend a couple of years getting to grips with those areas which are so important. They are important because I want you to take over here, and to do that in the coming years you will need to know how to run a business, not just to ride a horse, and round up cattle."

Cedric sat back and waited for the explosion. He didn't have to wait long.

"Bloody Hell Dad, you want me to go to the UK about which I know nothing very much, and go to school at my age, live in a foreign country with my Auntie, and mix with snotty nosed kids who couldn't know which end of a cow was its arse!"

Cedric sat quietly and let Craig, blow off steam.

"Only for a couple of years, Craig you will be pleased, and well equipped to look after things when you come back."

"Well I'm certainly not doing that dad, I think the sun has affected you or something, what does mum say about this bloody nonsense."

"She is in full agreement with only your future in her heart, at the very least it will curtail your rather colourful vocabulary," he said dryly.

"Well I'm not going." Craig got up and stomped out.

It took Brett to change his mind. A he left the house with

his head hung low, as near to tears as he had ever been, Brett, was sitting on the porch, polishing his boots.

He looked up, "Christ you look as though you lost a Dollar and found a zag."

"Dad wants to send me to England."

"I know."

"Well I'm not going and that's that."

"Good idea mate means you'll be galloping about on horseflesh for the rest of your life, getting laid in Darwin once a week, drinking yourself to an early grave, and finishing up like these lay-abouts trying to earn a buck."

Craig looked at him, expecting the usual cheeky grin. It wasn't there. For once, Brett was serious.

"Not for you the chance to see the world a bit, enjoy what is a beautiful Country, especially when the fucking sun shines (usually on a Thursday, once a month) meet a load of proper people, get yourself a real girl friend and learn how to conduct a business deal with the parasites who will try and take this place away from you when times get tough, especially when your dad is either, not here anymore, or is past it. You're a man now, physically anyway, but still a boy at heart with no problems about the future, no worries about other people, and no cares about this place. The place that your dad, and I, and these guys," he gestured towards the Station, "and you, have worked hard to make it; the up and coming Station in the Territory. Wish to God I'd had the chance you've got."

He bent down to pull his newly shined boots on. Got up and started to walk away.

Craig looked after him. He idolized Brett, respected his honesty and stature. It hurt to have him speak like that. In his heart he knew Brett, was right. But to leave his home and his friends and parents for two years or more, he went to find Jarra. Jarra listened to Craig's tale of woe and said nothing until Craig sat, dejected and sullen.

"With my people it is different," he said quietly, "when a boy is old enough his Grandfather takes over his life. He takes the boy into, '*The Dreaming,*' that is the land of our ancestors. There he lives as his ancestors, lived and he learns from his Grandfather, as his Grandfather, learned from his own Grandfather. He learns of the religion of his people, of the coming together of his people, the culture that has never changed in thousands of years. He learns of those many things I have taught you, how to find water, how to catch, and find food, how to exist in this vast and angry land, and many other ways of life. It becomes a sacred duty for Grandparents to do the same for their Grandchildren so that the Aborigine way of life never dies. To go into the '*Dreaming*' is what your father wishes for you. It is his love for you that makes him do this thing, so that you become a man with a man's knowledge, a mans morals and substance, a man to be proud, and able to mould his children. An Aborigine would never, and could never, refuse his entry into the '*Dreaming.*' You must not refuse this, Craig. I shall miss you, we shall all miss you, but it will be a joyful homecoming in a short time. Go with your God Craig."

Jarra seemed to float away, he was gone when Craig, lifted his head.

So Craig went to England.

Chapter 17

ENGLAND

He managed to get a seat on a Cargo plane which took priority over commercial flights, and had been given the all clear to use the one runway which had avoided destruction by the Cyclone. As he landed at Kai Tak Airport it seemed the plane would demolish a huge section of the property, and buildings, which loomed ahead as the plane circled across Victoria Harbour and approached from the sea. His fears were unfounded, and it landed without incident. Confined to the Airport as a transit passenger, he was at a loss as to his next move, so he asked an attractive Chinese girl behind the Information desk where he was to go from there. She smiled and looked at his travel documents.

"You need to board the plane at Gate number 54, but not yet, you have 2 hours to wait. There is a good Kiosk over there." She pointed towards it. "Get yourself some coffee and a sandwich, or if you wish something more substantial, it is a long flight to Heathrow. Are you on your own?"

"I'm afraid so," Craig pulled a face, "alone and lonely, perhaps not for long though." His eyes twinkled.

The flight was indeed a long one, nine hours. He was tired and the flight took off at 2200 hours so he settled down in his business class seat and slept most of the way. It was 2pm when he finally arrived at Heathrow, disoriented by the time difference he was bemused by the massive airport, and more people than he had ever seen in one place. He followed the other passengers like a forlorn sheep, through Passport Control to the baggage collection carousel and finally into Customs, where he passed un-noticed, and unmolested, into the main hallway. He had never met his Aunt Maud, merely seen a photograph some ten, or more years old. There were crowds waiting to greet the passengers and men with name boards announcing they were seeking certain people. He looked around but saw no-one who even resembled Aunt Maud. Suddenly he heard a squeal and a formidable woman with a rosy round face and very ample proportions who burst through the crowd shouting.

"Craig...Craigey over here ....Ooo- ooh."

That's got to be her, thought Craig, he waved and walked towards her. Before he knew it he was enveloped in her arms and pressed close to her very ample chest.

"I knew it must be you," she said, "They don't wander around here in January in shorts and cowboy hats. My, what a fine lad you are, I only saw you when you were a baby, such a lovely tan, to be that colour over here it must be rust." She chortled and gripped his arm, marching away towards the car park.

"It's so lovely to have you here, such a credit to your father. We had some lovely times together, he, and I when we were young. How is he?" Craig got no chance to tell her, she was off again. "My car is over here, little Morris Minor, not very big but goes like a dream, hang on, have to pay here." She fumbled in her handbag and pushed coins into a machine which spat out the amended ticket.

"Now we are ok takes for ages to get out of here but won't be long, when we do."

Craig had a job to wriggle his frame into the passenger seat and wrestled with the seat belt. "Must put that on, Police fine you here if it isn't fitted." They drove out of the car park, Craig, bewildered by the road signs and traffic lights.

"Thought we would take a diversion to show you where your school is, lovely school, not far from home, Lucky your Grandfather was able to get you in there."

She swung the car into a right hand turn which was signposted Winchester, and buzzed along the tarmac road, which was another new innovation for, Craig being used to dirt roads in the main. After about an hour, during which, Maud, delighted in giving a commentary on the places of interest, they came into the main City dominated by the Cathedral. Craig after a while let her chat away his thoughts a tangle, wondering how he would ever get used to such a vast change in his world.

"There, on your right, that's Bramington Grammar School."

There was a vast expanse of playing field, with rugby posts and a pavilion, and a huge imposing building as a backdrop. The architecture was beautiful and glowed in the late sunshine. Craig was entranced.

"Will I live there?" he asked.

"Certainly not, you will live with me. You can cycle to school, most of the pupils do, except those with very rich parents who drive them in their flashy cars, just to show off really. Oh, no, I want to make a fuss of you while I can."

She beamed a huge smile at him. Craig decided she was really a lovely lady, and cheered up a bit. Her house was a large Tudor style detached two storey building set back from a circular drive which was covered in gravel. Maud crunched to a stop and grabbed Craig's case before he could do so, marching in through the front door into a wide and attractive hallway. The place was large.

"You live here alone Auntie?" asked Craig.

"Yes, never had the chance to meet the right man got a lot of friends and a little girl who comes in twice a week to help with the chores. I am very busy though, President of the local book club, and I look after the Village in Bloom society, we make sure our village is lovely in the summer, full of blossom and clean as a whistle. We won the first prize four times." She beamed. "Now, you must be starved poor lamb. Let me show you your room, you can have a bath if you like, and I will get some good English food ready. But a cup of tea would be nice before that."

His room was large and nicely furnished with a comfortable bed, table and chair, and a settee across one wall. Colourful curtains at a window which looked out across a substantial garden. There was a radio and a bookcase full of books. A large freestanding wardrobe was empty apart from a dozen or so hangers, and two extra blankets folded neatly on the upper shelf. The bathroom was immediately opposite, and housed a huge yellow bath. Craig viewed this with some concern. He was used to showering beneath an upturned dustbin lid, punctured with holes, and fed from the water tower with a force that knocked you off of your feet, if you weren't careful. He shrugged and just washed himself and went downstairs carefully. Cups and saucers were arranged on the table with a flowery tablecloth and the teapot was covered with what, Craig, mistakenly decided was an old hat, dispensed scalding hot tea. He looked around at the knick knacks on the shelves and mantelpiece. There were dried flowers in a vase and a huge green plant in the window. He smiled to himself; it's the Old Country all right. He tucked into a chocolate biscuit. Later, Maud, provided a huge steak and kidney pudding with all the trimmings. Full, and tired, Craig went to bed wondering whether or not he was in a trance. Maud phoned, Cedric, and told him, Craig had arrived and she would look after him. Maud dropped Craig, off at School on his first day. Previously he had been dragged around the shops where Maud, had bought the school uniform, long grey flecked trousers, a matching jacket, a crimson blazer with the school crest on the pocket, shirts and underwear and the crowning glory, a straw boater.

Craig protested, "I'm certainly not wearing that thing," He complained, "I'll be the laughing stock."

"No you won't, all the boys wear them its tradition, anyway that's not until the summer term. You must wear your cap though. The Headmaster insists on that. Anyway you will look very smart."

Craig looked critically at the cap, and at the long trousers, he'd never worn anything but shorts, and grieved over the loss of his blonde wavy hair, now cut to a traditional short back and sides, and it was cold around his neck. He sighed, nothing he could do without upsetting Aunt Maud, and he didn't want to do that. The first day he did very little, allocated a House, whatever that meant, and a locker in the changing rooms, introduced to his Form Teacher, a gaunt looking tall man with a stoop, wearing a gown of black which was presumably to protect his suit, not that it needed protecting, it looked as though it was 50 years old. The other lads, who were around Craig's age looked at him with a superior attitude and no-one, spoke to him. He found the morning depressing, and found a seat in the dining hall at lunch time on his own. The food was plentiful and moderately good, and he spent his time summing up the other boys. He wasn't impressed. Lunch was followed by an hours break, and, Craig wandered out onto the playing field. it was a bright sunny day, there, groups kicked a ball around and generally engaging in horseplay. His attention was drawn to a group roughing up a smaller boy who was obviously getting the worst of things. Craig wandered closer.

"Come on now shell out your pocket money you little weed."

A fat larger boy had hold of the lads hair and was shaking him. The other were laughing and egging him on.

"I don't have any pocket money." His spectacles dropped to the ground.

"Of course you do, daddy wouldn't leave you with no money."

Craig walked over. "Leave him alone" he said quietly.

"Oh I say, this is the criminal from Down Under lads! Do you know the difference between an Australian, and a Kangaroo?"

"No." Said the lads.

"Nor do I, they look the same, just as ugly." They all laughed.

"Leave him alone, or I shall bloody deck you," said Craig, quietly, walking nearer to fat boy.

"Like to see you try."

Craig walked over and hit him hard on the side of his head. Fat boy dropped like a stone, his eyes rolling back, and his mouth gaping open with shock. The others went silent.

"Anyone else want to argue the bloody toss?" Craig turned to face them. "Leave this lad alone or I'll clobber the lot of you."

They ran off leaving the fat boy squirming on the ground. Taking the small lad by the arm, Craig walked him away. "Are you ok, did he hurt you?"

"No, thank you so much, they are always picking on me and taking my pocket money, they make my life a misery." he brushed himself down and picked up his spectacles.

"I'm Craig, Craig Weston, if there is any more bullying from them tell me."

My name is Charles, Charles Forsyth, I am most awfully grateful. You've just started haven't you, first day?"

Craig grinned, has to be Charles he thought. "Yep, first day, got into trouble without trying."

"If I can help in any way Craig, They call me a bit of a swat because I love schoolwork, so if you need any help at any time, I'm sure you won't," he added hurriedly," but if I can."

"Well that's very good of you, I've never been to school before, had to learn by wireless, you know being taught by a disembodied voice coming from a loudspeaker. All very well, but difficult."

"I bet it is." Charles was shocked. "Any time then, I would love to help."

And help he did, the reputation, Craig had earned stood Charles, in good stead, he was not made the object of ridicule again and, Charles was a light at the end of Craig's tunnel. Even though he paid attention in class, Craig fretted for the life he had left behind. He longed for space and anything energetic. He made up his mind that whilst he would in deference to his father, do all he could to learn that which was available but to keep his body fit and active he would concentrate on sport. He would get out of bed at 6am. Even though it was still dark he would run 5 miles before returning for one of Maud's breakfasts. He enjoyed the cycle ride to school even though he had more trouble learning how to ride the thing than he ever had breaking in a horse. On the Rugby field he became a force to be reckoned with, ploughing his way through the defending line and rarely failing to score a Try, a drop kick came naturally to him, and he glowed as the ball sailed high between the posts.

Gradually the attitude towards him changed and he became a bit of a hero and was carried shoulder high from the field after a particularly good win. Life became enjoyable and he settled in to living with Aunt Maud, who was delighted when Charles, came round for tea and to spend a couple of hours with Craig, easing him through the academic aspect of their shared existence. As spring arrived he began to revel in the English weather and the glory of spring, life was good. He spent as much time as he could, visiting, John, and Mary, conscious of the fact that his trip and school fees were paid by them, and the obvious delight they felt on his visits. On one or two occasions Aunt Maud, drove him over to Hadleigh Hall where she was made very welcome. She marvelled at the splendour of the building and furnishings and chatted away continuously.

Craig pulled on his trainers and shrugged into his sweat shirt. He set off on the morning run, it was 6.00am the sun was just yawning and peeping above the skyline. Shadows from the trees slanted horizontally across the landscape, and the faint rays picked out the silver leaves of the birch. Craig loved this time of the day, there was a peaceful and clean aura about it, which an hour before, had seemed dead, and unfathomable in the darkness. He jogged out of the grounds and on to the country lane turning left to meet the rising Sun. He ran at a leisurely pace sucking in the fresh, crisp air, and hummed a tune as he went. It was some half mile further that she, appeared from an adjoining lane. Dressed in tight shorts and a sloppy sweat top, her hair was dark and flowing and held in place by a colourful head- band. Unaware of Craig, she jogged at a steady pace, her long legs moving easily and her tight buttocks moving tantalizingly. Craig slowed down and ran behind her for a few minutes enjoying the view. She still hadn't heard him due to a Sony Walkman clipped to her belt, the microphone plugged in one ear. Craig caught up with her and appeared on her right. Startled she looked at him her eyes slanted with concern. What eyes thought Craig, violet, like Elizabeth Taylor, her features were perfect, and Craig grinned.

" G'day," he said.

Pulling the microphone out of her ear she said, "What?"

"I said G'day…names Craig."

"You must be Australian?" She said disinterested.

"Dinkie Die Aussie That's me," Craig put on his friendliest smile.

"Well, never mind… not your fault." She put her microphone back in her ear and speeded up.

Craig speeded up with her. The girl stopped. Turning towards him she glared at him. "I come out at this time of the day to get a bit of peace, not to waste my time jogging along with a throw out from the Antipodes. Now do you mind, either go ahead or fall behind. In other words Bugger off!"

Craig looked hurt, "I was just looking for some company, not to be a nuisance, shame you Brits are so unfriendly… anyway you are not running properly."

He fell back and stopped, looking crestfallen. The girl ran on a few steps and then stopped, she turned with her hands on her hips, her lips thinned into a tight line.

"What the Hell do you mean I am not running properly?"

"You are on your toes too much, wear yourself out too soon. You need to get your whole foot on the ground use your calves to push you along."

"I suppose you're an expert?"

"Race you to the post box, see who breathes properly."

"What post box?"

"About a mile ahead…give you a minute's start."

The girl glowered at him, hesitated… "You are on."

Turning, she set off, arms tucked in and thrusting like pistons. Craig grinned and waited a full minute, she was 300 yards ahead, he burst into a full blooded run, memories of Jarra Bulla goading him from years ago ."Longer strides, deeper breath, you run like a woman."

Craig swept past her; the post box was 150 yards ahead and, Craig, leaned against it breathing quietly. She stopped beside him, breathing heavily and doing her best to control her lungs.

"Are you alright?" He looked concerned doing his best not to grin.

"I am perfectly all right thank you." She hoped she spoke without puffing. Her face was set and cross.

"Oh come on," said Craig, "Don't be mad with me. I mean no harm…just like to be friends," What's your name?"

She hesitated…he really was quite a hunk, strong, good looking.

She relented, "Mariette, Mariette Shaw," she said, "You are pretty fast on your feet." And in other ways she thought. "I must go, need to be home by seven."

Craig nodded, "Can I see you again, jog together tomorrow? About the same time. I'll wait by the lane you came out of back there," He pointed his thumb over his shoulder.

"Well ok." Mariette smiled for the first time and her face lit up, "You can teach me how to run properly. No racing though."

Craig watched her jog back; she looked over her shoulder just once and disappeared around the bend.

Craig was there early the next morning, "mustn't look too eager," he thought. After ten minutes he decided she wasn't going to show, and about to set off, she appeared. Mariette smiled, secretly pleased to see him, but not intending to let him know that. They jogged along together without speaking for a while until Craig, looked at her and said.

"Well, come on, tell me about you."

"What do you want to know, nosey?" she retorted.

"Everything."

She raised her eyebrows. "Such as?"

"How old are you?"

"What ?" she glowered at him. "Don't you know it is about the most rude question you can ask woman?"

"You are not a woman," grinned Craig. "You are as beautiful as the sunrise, fresh as a new spring daffodil…..young as a new born lamb….no way has womanhood taken hold yet."

Mariette stopped dead. "Christ I've heard some chat up lines but that takes the bloody biscuit." She was gob smacked but glowed inside. He meant what he said. His eyes were serious, no smirk…just honest. She shook her head and started to jog again.

"Where did you get that bullshit from?"

"Not bullshit….just how you look to me." Craig jogged along looking straight ahead.

After a few minutes of silence, "I'm 17." She muttered.

"Beat you, I'm 18!" They both laughed.

After that they both relaxed and chatted openly. She was interested in Australia, intrigued with the life he described, he told her of Jarra, and the Cyclone, of the blazing Sun and the 'Big wet' of his parents, and life of the Station…how he missed it, but still loved the Old Country.

Mariette told him of her parents who had a large farm, mainly cattle…Jersey Cows and a huge Jersey bull named Henry. Two cats and a Border Collie called Martha. An older Sister, Deborah and two horses…Bill and Ben. Too soon it was time to call it a day. They arranged to meet again the next morning. Both parted with their own thoughts.

"Do you ride?" Mariette asked a few days later.

"I grew up with horses, why."

"Not horses….bikes."

Oh yes I have a bike, my Aunt Maude, bought me a Dawes, I ride it to School every day."

"Good….meet you here on Saturday. We'll go for a picnic, and you can come to meet mum and dad and stay for dinner."

Taken aback, Craig stammered, "Is that a good idea? I mean they don't know me."

"Why d'you think you're coming to dinner?"

I suppose dad is going to approve me. Make sure I'm not an under able from down under, thought Craig.

"Don't worry, they won't eat you," giggled Mariette, seeing his worried look, "they just want to make sure you haven't got two heads."

"Ha! Ha!." He put out his tongue.

They met up on Saturday morning, Mariette arriving on a sit up and beg bike with a bulging basket in front of the handlebars. She was dressed in a cream sun-dress, her hair tied back with a big blue bow. She looked delicious thought Craig, and said so. The morning was glorious, fresh, warm and quiet. As they pedaled along the lanes, Mariette's long brown legs flashing and distracting Craig. After about half an hour Mariette called.

" Here we are," she pulled up and jumped off. "We walk now," she said and lifted her bike over a low dry stone wall into a field. Craig followed her towards a copse of trees. Suddenly they were in a grassy glade by the river. The water gurgled and chuckled, disturbed occasionally by a fish surfacing to swallow a fly or some other unlucky insect. The water was as clear as crystal. Craig had never seen such a peaceful and lovely scene.

"How ever did you find this place?" He asked, "I suppose you bring all your boyfriends here?"

"Usually two or three at a time... just in case I get bored."

Craig lifted the basket off her bike and Mariette; spread a rug in the sunshine flickering through the branches. Then she lay down flat on her back. "Better than dusty Oz."

"We too have beauty spots, but not like this." He was looking at her. With her hands behind her head, her young breasts, pert and full, he felt a stirring in his loins and thighs. He tried to shake it off with no effect.

"Are you queer?" Mariette asked with a bland expression.

"WHAT!" Craig was shocked rigid. "What did you say?"

"Queer..You know, Nancy Boy, rather be with other men and boys."

"Whatever gave you that idea?" Craig, looked so devastated that Mariette chuckled.

"Well we have known each other for about two months and you haven't tried to kiss me once."

Craig stood open mouthed. "I didn't want to spoil something very wonderful," he muttered.

"For God's sake, come here you silly arse." she grinned.

Craig leaned over and kissed her gently and she slid her arms around his neck and pulled him close, kissing him back with a passion that took him aback. He felt himself stirring and a bit breathless, but the desire took over and they lay together kissing and hugging. Mariette undid his shirt and slid her hands around him pulling him close, entwining herself, her lips parted and a soft probing tongue pushed all the reserve from him. He caressed her breasts, feeling the nipples harden, and pressed his mouth against them. She wriggled closer and sighed. Urgently she undid the belt of his shorts a slid them down. She consumed him completely and she guided him into her, kissing him hard and pulling him close. The explosion of passion was something, Craig, had never experienced. He fell back gasping, and Mariette rolled on top of him, they lay unspeaking, enjoying each other as, Craig felt a need arising again. They made love in the sun and explored one another's bodies, the time passed unnoticed.

"That was your first time wasn't it?" Mariette grinned, she lay spread-eagled her dress high around her waist exposing her slender body, and long legs. Craig couldn't take his eyes off her. "Me too," she said. "Good wasn't it?"

Craig looked at her suspiciously, "How come you're so good at it then?"

"Instinct. Comes naturally, I think it will catch on." She jumped up straightening her dress. Grabbing her bike she set off. "Come on we'll be late for dinner."

Craig set off after her, until a sudden thought struck him. He stopped and looked worried to death.

"What's up?" Mariette looked worried.

"I never thought," stammered Craig, "I never took any precautions. What if ?"

"Mariette laughed... "Good job I did then isn't it?"

Craig relaxed, his eyes narrowed, "You planned all this you hussy didn't you?"

"What a shocking thing to say." Mariette pulled a playful face and her eyes sparkled. "Aren't you glad?" She pedaled off as fast as she could, Craig pedaling after her, and, catching her up he pulled her off her bike and kissed her. Both laughing they sat on a dry stone wall to catch their breath. They kissed again to the disgust of two spinster ladies with dogs who were passing.

"Disgusting," one said loudly, "No shame," Mariette stuck her tongue out and they toppled back off the wall into the long grass.

They made love again. "Much more of this and, I shall fall in love with you," she murmured.

"I already am in love with you."

Mariette looked at him, his eyes were serious. He meant it.

They arrived at the farm and met a tall, and attractive woman in breeches and a tartan shirt, she was blonde and wore her hair pulled back tied with a ribbon in a pony tail. She was carrying a bucket full of an indescribable sludge.

"Hi Deb," Mariette called, "This is Craig, Craig, my sister, Deborah."

Deborah grinned at Craig. "So you're the reason Mariette,

can't sleep, heard so much about you I was convinced you came from Olympus. See you at dinner, must feed the pigs."

She walked off along the path, "Mariette," she called over her shoulder, "you'd better get rid of that dress before Mum sees it." She grinned to herself, 'about bloody time she thought. Mariette blushed and pulled her dress round. A tell tale blood stain was obvious at the back.

"Oh Christ." She scampered off and shot up the stairs to her room.

Craig, left alone, walked slowly to the door and tentatively stepped into the hallway. He was greeted by a tall, and heavily built woman with rosy cheeks and a warm friendly smile.

"You must be Craig, Welcome to our home. Mariette has told us all about you."

"So pleased to meet you Mrs. Shaw."

"Wonder she hasn't put an article in the paper," said Craig, "Deborah has also been given all the details." Mrs. Shaw laughed.

"I'll show you to your room Craig, thought you would like to have a wash and brush up before dinner. Dinner is nearly ready, come down when you're done and have a glass of Cider…we brew it ourselves you know."

Craig had just had a shower and changed his shirt when there was a tap on the door. Mariette stood there fresh as a daisy with a change of dress. She ran in and kissed Craig.

"Come on down and meet pops, you'll like him, everybody does."

Mr. Shaw was, in Craig's eyes the epitome of an English Farmer. A big jovial man with thinning fair hair a hint of grey at the temples and laughing brown eyes. He had a broad West Country accent.

"Pleased to meet you son." he said. "I've …"

"Heard a lot about me, "interrupted Craig, smiling "I'm very pleased to meet you too Sir..."

Dinner was massive, a huge joint of roasted pork, obviously a departed member of the farm with crackling and roasted potatoes, green vegetables, also home grown, and all the trimmings. A huge apple pie followed, with cream. Mariette was bubbling, chattering away and stealing loving glances at Craig. Something had changed in Mariette, and Deborah knew exactly what it was. Offered another piece of apple pie Craig declined, he was full up and said so.

"At least have a piece of fruit Craig," said Mrs. Shaw, "Mariette, pass Craig an apple, one of own crop."

"I think she has already passed Craig an apple." said Deborah dryly. Her mother frowned at her, and Mariette glared.

Later that evening, Mariette and Craig, wandered around the farm. There had been a litter of piglets born that day and, Mariette was like a child with them, giving them names and identities.

"Don't get too attached," Craig said, "Won't be long before they finish up on the dinner plate."

Mariette was shocked. "Callous, that's what you are." Craig grinned.

Indoors, Fred, and Ethel Shaw, lingered at the table, whilst Deborah, busied herself clearing the crockery.

"I've been noticing things," Fred said, "Looks to me that young Mariette is a bit sweet on Craig." He puffed on his pipe.

His Wife laughed, and Deborah giggled. "Not much gets past you Dad, does it?"

"Ah, that be right, young Craig, seems to be the same way if you think about it. Not a bad thing mind, fine lad that Craig. Don't know whether you've noticed mum?"

"Oh Yes, I've noticed Fred, I'm surprised you have taken so long to cotton on." Fred looked puzzled.

"Ah! Reckon I'm right."

Craig spent more and more time at the farm, during the break from the school year and enjoyed helping Fred, with the Farm. The physical work suited him and he got to stay overnight quite often. He had a room, only a few feet away from Mariette's. He was dozing off one night when there was a tap on the door. It opened and Mariette, crept in closing the door behind her. The moon cast a silver light across the room .Craig sat up, startled.

"What are you up to?" he said.

"Shhhhh! Just thought I'd come and tuck you in."

"If your Dad finds you here we're toast."

"He won't, I listened at their door. He's snoring, like one of his pigs."

She tip-toed across the room and snuggled into the bed bedside him. "Aren't you pleased to see me?"

Craig laughed, "Yes of course I am. Brazen little hussy." He kissed her and she wriggled close, nibbling his ear.

They made love that night, and for many nights to come firmly believing they had been undetected. Deborah however knew better but said nothing, secretly envying Mariette. Her love life had been disastrous, two lovers, each of whom had cheated on her. She had convinced herself that she was condemned to a life of spinsterhood.

Aunt Maud had some news from Australia, a letter addressed to both, she, and Craig. She was bubbling over when Craig came home.

"What do you think?" she said, "Such lovely news from your mother."

"What news?" asked Craig.

"You are going to have a brother or sister, your mum is pregnant, she has about 8 months to go, isn't that lovely?"

Craig wasn't sure. He was so used to being an only child. Why couldn't she have had another baby earlier; they would have been nearer in age to each other. Must have been a mistake he mused. He grinned, there's life in the old man yet. The letter contained news of the Ranch, all was going well, Darwin had almost recovered and business was back to normal and prospering. They all missed Craig, and wanted news of his life now that he had left school. He felt homesick. Since meeting Mariette, he had neglected to write as often, he felt guilty; nearly three years had passed since he left. He promised himself he would write that very evening. That night, snuggling into Mariette's arms, he made a decision.

"Are you awake?"

"Umm, I am now," She opened one eye, "What does my master desire as though I didn't know!"

"Will you marry me?"

Mariette sat upright. "What did you say?"

"I said, will you marry me because I love you very, very much."

"I'm still asleep, having a lovely dream; I dreamed you asked me to marry you! How good is that?"

"Well, will you?"

"It needs some thought, mustn't make snap decision, you will have to give me time." Craig's face fell.

Her face lit up in the moonlight, "That's it I've thought enough oh yes, my love, I will, I will." She squealed and hugged him.

"Shah, you'll wake em."

That morning Mariette was as lively as a cricket but had been threatened by Craig, not to say anything until he had done so. She was however so excited that Deborah and her parents, were a bit suspicious. Craig stood up when the chance arrived.

"There are a couple of things I would like to say please. As you know my mother, is going to have a baby later this year which is good news."

"'Ere ere," said Fred, lighting his pipe.

"On top of that I feel I should go home to Australia to see

them all. It has been nearly three years now and I really need to see them all."

Mariette looked startled. Craig had said nothing about going to Australia. Was he going for long, would he ever come back. Craig caught the look on her face.

"You certainly need to see them," said Ethel, "we can't keep you here, that would be unkind, although we shall miss you."

"There is something else," he looked at them both. "Mariette, and I, are in love, and we want to get married."

"What did I tell you." Fred grinned all over his face."I knew that was going to be the case, I know these things see. You ain't up the duff my girl are you?" he added as an afterthought.

"Certainly not!" Mariette looked shocked, "Whatever next?"

"We are delighted," said Ethel Shaw, "You both have our blessing, but I can't say it's a surprise."

"Thank you," said Craig. "This is the hard bit though, I want to marry Mariette, and take her with me to OZ, to meet my parents."

"Wow," said Mariette, "I thought you were going to stand me up."

This news rather shook Mariette's parents; they hadn't envisaged losing her so quickly. Craig saw the distress on their faces. He quickly went on. "It won't be for keeps, we will be back of course, I want my folks to meet Mariette, and for us to see the new arrival when he, or she puts in an appearance."

That seemed to relieve their fears and soon the three

women were deep into planning the wedding. They married at the local Church, an old, and established place of worship, set in a long time filled cemetery, which was beautifully kept by the villagers. The reception was at the farm on a glorious sunny day. Tables and chairs dotted the lawns and the food not only plentiful, but delicious, thanks to Ethel, and Aunt Maud, who was in her element. Fred spent his time supplying, and praising his own brand of Scrumpy, which had already threatened to incapacitate quite a few of the guests. It seemed the whole village had turned up, bringing gifts ranging from the inevitable toaster to three dozen goose eggs. The guests of honour were Craig's Grandparents, Sir. John, and Mary Hadleigh. In the eyes of the Village it was the same as having visited Royalty, and established, Craig as the Squire of the Manor. The whole of the afternoon resembled an episode from "The Darling buds of May," and was one of the happiest day of Craig, and Mariette's life. As they left Mariette, sought out Deborah. She found her sitting outside the cowshed. She was in tears.

"Oh! Debs whatever is the matter?" Mariette hugged her, "Don't cry on my Wedding Day."

Deborah sniffed and wiped her eyes."I'm so happy for you, I'm sorry Mariette, I didn't want to cry but I can't help it. I shall miss you so much."

"It won't be long before you are all dressed in white, you'll see. The right guy will be along, all the more special because it's taken him so long to get here. Come on big sister, come and see us off."

As they left in the Rolls Mariette, took careful aim and made sure that, Deborah, caught her bouquet. She watched her hug it tightly as though she would never let it go. They flew to Jersey for their honeymoon, where Sir. John, had booked them into the *Pomme dor Hotel* and arranged for an all expenses paid for the fortnight. It was August and the traditional Battle of Flowers took place whilst they were there, they bathed, and spent hours on the beach finding a quiet, and secluded place behind the jutting rocks. They danced at night in the many night spots and ate so much seafood that Mariette swore she was growing fins. It was over too soon, but the prospect of their trip to Australia filled their minds. It was early September that they flew out of Heathrow, bound for Darwin both quiet with their own thoughts, and wondering what the future would bring.

Chapter 18

TREASURED...

Mariette was overwhelmed at the place. She had never dreamed it would be as hot, nor as desolate. Everyone was at the airport to meet them, including, Brett. Jarra had stayed behind not willing to risk his life in those man-made death traps that belched smoke, and shook the flesh off your bones. Janine, and Mariette hit it off at once, and Craig, hugged his father, with sheer joy at being back. They had a drink at the Airport, the bar opened only when an aircraft landed, and piled into the Ute. Brett co-erced Mariette, into Tinker, much to Craig's concern, and away they went into a new future. At the Ranch Ho Chin had prepared a large spread of his favourite dishes outside beneath a huge Marquee, and over lunch they caught up on each-others news. Brett, showed, Mariette around the Ranch and, Craig, spent time with his mother and father. Mariette met all the Ranch hands and liked them all. At one stage Mariette clung on to Brett's arm.

"There's a Zulu over there by the paddock," she said. "He's got a spear or something, and he looks a bit warlike."

"Brett laughed, "He's no Zulu, that's Jarra. Jarra Bull, pure bred Aborigine. One of us, Craig's best mate. He's all dressed up to welcome you, I guess."

Jarra walked over and grinned at Mariette, his face was transformed when he grinned, his large white teeth and twinkling eyes lighting up his face. "G'day, you must be Mariette, welcome to S'tralia."

Mariette put out her hand, tentatively, "How do you do."

"He won't eat you," said Brett, "at least not today."

Craig appeared. "Jarra!" He shouted running across, He hugged Jarra. Standing back Jarra, looked at Craig, with true affection.

"You left as a boy Craig, you return as a man. Welcome home." He, and Craig, walked away.

"He's got a bone through his nose?" Marietta looked shocked. "And funny things hanging from his belt."

"That's his lunch." Brett said enjoying her puzzled look.

Cedric, and, Janine showed Mariette, to her room and showed her the layout of the house.

"Could I have a shower?" She asked, "If you have one, it's a bit hot."

"Of course," Janine said.

To Mariette's surprise, Janine led her outside, and across to the water tower. There was a corrugated iron enclosure open at the tower side.

"When you're ready, stand in the middle and pull on the chain. Nice and private, I'll bring you a robe and some towels."

Mariette laughed, "Now I know I'm in Australia."

A few minutes later there was a scream from the shower, she pulled the chain and a deluge of water poured over her through the perforate dustbin lid. Craig ran over and laughed. She stood there like a drowned rat gasping.

"I've never been so wet in all my life," she said. "Go away!"

Later they were all sitting in the cool of the lounge, enjoying some iced lemonade, Mariette, was examining everything, and admiring the furniture and the Knick-Knacks which adorned the walls and shelves. She picked up the stone from the mantelpiece.

"What's this Cedric?" She asked frowning and feeling the weight of the stone.

"That was picked up by Caliph, when we nearly got buried by the Cyclone, got stuck in the frog of his hoof; sent him lame for a while, I kept it as a souvenir."

Mariette said nothing but walked over to the kitchen and returned with a glass of water. She dropped the stone into the water, swirled it around and took it out, placing it on the table.

"What do you see?" She said.

"A wet stone," said Craig.

"No it's not, its bone dry." Mariette disagreed. She walked outside and came back with a similar size pebble. She dropped that in the glass, and then took it out."That's a wet stone."

So," said Craig puzzled.

"The only stone that sheds water, won't get wet is a diamond." She paused for effect.

There was a silence in the room. Brett, and Cedric, came to the table and looked at the stone.

"Are you saying this is a diamond?" asked Cedric.

"It certainly is," said Mariette, "It's a big diamond, and, as far as I can see it is a blue/white, can't say for sure, needs an expert to value it."

"What's it worth?" asked Janine.

"When cut properly, polished and set in a gold ring for example, about 50 or 60."

"Enough for a night out for all of us." said Brett.

"Thousand." Said Mariette quietly.

"What, are you saying that 50 or 60 thousand dollars has been sitting on the bloody mantelpiece for over 3 years?"

"Pounds," grinned Mariette, "Pounds sterling, real money."

"How do you know all this?" Craig asked.

"When I was at College I had a part time job in the Library, made a few pounds to help with my books. Still kept the job after I left school. It was boring, nothing much to do, so I read books. I can't be bothered with trashy novels so I read about all sorts of things, including diamonds, a girls best friend you know."

Cedric was dumbfounded to think that the early days at the Ranch had been a very tight financial existence and all that money had been sitting there waiting.

"Tell me the story of the Cyclone." said Mariette.

Craig went through it in detail, the devastation, the mine collapsing, and the disintegration of the mountain and the sludge from which Caliph picked up the stone.

"It is very unusual for there to be an isolated diamond, there must be more, perhaps a lot more, where this one came from."

"Apparently the mine was worked for years, tunnels criss-crossing beneath the ground, and nothing ever came out of it."

"Weren't they mining for Gold?"

"Yes, but they never found any, nor any diamonds."

"Not surprised, you rarely find the two together." Mariette looked thoughtful. "Diamonds are found in what they call the Blue, It is a mother lode running through the strata of rock. Very hard stuff," she said. "From what you tell me, the mine collapsed into itself and half the mountain fell on top of it."

Craig nodded.

"Well that's where the diamonds are, no longer in the mountain but spread across the land in the sludge, sure to be some, not necessarily all as big as this beauty."

"We must get this thing valued." said Craig.

"That is a problem," Mariette said solemnly." If you present this at the assay office, he will want to know where it came from. There is a widespread illicit diamond market and the only way to avoid being suspected is to tell the truth. Then you will have the world, and his wife, descending on you and the place will be bedlam. The best place to get a proper valuation is from the Big guns, the Diamond mining Companies in Perth. They will also want to know where it came from and they won't believe you. It would involve investigation and legal clap trap, because a diamond mine does not exist here."

"I do know a guy who would give us a valuation, for a price. A German who was sacked from De Beers, in South Africa. He was deeply involved in illicit diamond smuggling. Crooked as a Banyan tree." Said Brett.

"Hardly likely to give you a truthful valuation." said Cedric.

"Only if he got paid a percentage of the ultimate sale, whenever that was."

"Where is he?" asked Craig.

"Papua, New Guinea, Head hunting country."

"Charming," remarked Janine dryly. "What if we mined it ourselves? Just a matter of sifting through the sludge."

Brett laughed, "There are hundreds of tons of the stuff, and it isn't sludge any more, hard as nails now it has dried out. We haven't got the manpower or the equipment, nor the money to buy gear or hire the manpower."

"Alright," said Mariette, "We declare the facts to the assay office, produce the diamond as proof, and sell claims, declare the area to be a diamond hot spot. Let the others do the digging. How big is the area?"

"Including the rest of the mountain, and the mine, or at least the surface above where the mine was, 500 acres, give or take."

"Right that's $50,000 for doing nothing at $100 a claim. That way we are in the clear, the big guns will be here in no time and so will the rest of Oz I expect. We would also get a true valuation and even sell this rock for what it's worth. In the meantime we tell no-one, not a soul outside this room, if it gets out before we do the right thing, we are in the crap." Mariette beamed.

"Where the hell did you find this beautiful little gem?" asked Brett. "She' got more brains than the rest of us put together."

Mariette beamed even more. "I'm a woman."

The next day, Cedric, Brett, Craig, and Mariette, all went into Darwin to the Assay office.

"You do not want to sell Mr. Weston?" The clerk asked urgently.

"No," smiled Cedric, just wanted to show this young lady the extent of the land, she's come to join us, just married to my son."

"Congratulations," the clerk muttered, not totally convinced. He pulled a roll of drawings out of the drawer and spread them on the desk top. Cedric pored over the map. He pointed out the location of the Ranch.

"Our land stretches east, across here to the other side of where there used to be a Gold mine, it then goes south in a straight line for 30 miles. Bordered across the Northern limit by the mountains and way across from the Ranch to the west. Large area, right?" he addressed the clerk.

"Certainly is, old man Dorovic sold it too cheaply, I said so at the time."

"He was well pleased, still is." Said Brett. "Anyway, down to business, he produced the diamond. "What do you think of that?"

Not really interested, the clerk pushed his spectacles back up his nose and peered at the stone. He looked up, and then polished his glasses on his handkerchief and looked again.

"Is this what I think it is?" he said, his voice trembling. "A diamond, it is a very big stone, where did you get this?"

"If you give me your word that what I am about to tell you goes no further than this office. I assure you there is no illegal aspect, nothing that is underhand, just that which we need to do is the right thing."

Cedric locked his eyes into that of the clerk, who nodded dumbly. Cedric then outlined the whole history of the diamond find, including the fact that the stone had sat on the mantelpiece for three years before Mariette had recognized it.

"So, can we sell off claims through you, or is there more to it than that?"

The Clerk walked around the desk and locked the front door. He hung up a closed sign and indicated that all of them went through to his back room.

"There is a great deal more to it than that Mr. Weston, There are very stringent laws appertaining to the mining of diamonds. The whole of Australia's diamond industry is controlled by the Argyle Diamond Company, now in Perth. They are responsible for one third of the world's natural supply. As such, the mining and distribution of gems, is rigidly supervised. Were there to be a surge of diamonds into the world market, the value and price would be seriously affected. Consequently no mining can be authorized without a rigid investigation by their specialists. Before you can do anything else you must inform them of that which you have told me. They will visit and inspect the site, evaluate the stone, and advise you of the situation. I have no authority other than advising you. Please believe me when I say our conversation will be entirely confidential."

"Just for interest what do you think this diamond could be worth?" Mariette asked sweetly.

"It depends on many things, first the clarity, if there are no flaws or debris, if it is a blue/white or pink even, if it will cut with a minimum of waste, and judging by the size at the moment, if it falls within the highest grade. Based on these 'ifs' it could range between $60,000 and $100,000 or, with the finest treatment and the right buyer, a million is not out of the question. I can only wish you good fortune, and the assurance that the Argyle Co. will give you a fair, and honest deal."

They took their leave.

"As Del Boy' would say, we could all be Miyonaires." chuckled Mariette.

Chapter 19

FLAWLESS

The Argyle Company wasted no time; within a week three of their senior men flew into Darwin, and arrived at the Ranch in a hired limousine. They listened attentively, saying very little and asked to see the site. The story was related to them and they carefully examined the diamond.

"There is, of course no guarantee that other stones exist, one swallow doesn't make a summer."

"Are young English? Asked Cedric.

"No Dutch," he replied. "We have the same little sayings as you, however, on the face of it, I would think there is an excellent chance that there could be. We shall test the ground to see if there is any sign of kimberlite which is the normal host of diamonds, or even of lamproite, an even better host. With your permission we will take your diamond for expert examination, we will give you a receipt of course, and our geologists will be here within the week with a written description and valuation. Don't look worried our credentials are impeccable. This phone number will connect to our Head Office in Perth, please check us out."

"We sure will." said Mariette.

True to their word in a few days a large white van with, "Argyle Diamond Company," arrived at the Ranch with three men who asked to be shown the site. They said very little, but unloaded a surprisingly complex set of equipment, assuring, Cedric that they would have a recommendation within an hour or two. The highlight was the estimated value of their diamond. In brief it was assessed as being large enough to allow cutting with 58 facets. The geologist explained in more detail.

"At this stage it appears to be absolutely colourless. No internal inclusions, or imperfections, thus it has been assessed as FL (Flawless) It weighs 12 carats which would reduce to around 10 when cut. These findings have been determined by high quality X Rays and sophisticated equipment, but it must be born in mind that, during cutting there could be variations. Currently the market would indicate a value of at least £85,000 but there would be charges for cutting, polishing and, depending upon the ultimate setting if any of £3,000 plus of course charges for service by Argyle of £2,000. At the same time it may well be that a private buyer would pay well in excess of that figure, if a setting of their choice proved to be more elaborate."

"Around £80 Grand then?" Said Cedric.

The geologist nodded. "Quite a find Mr. Weston."

The geologist's investigation took longer than they expected and it was nearly dark when they finished. They returned to the Ranch, and the chief honcho sat himself down to explain.

"We can't assess the diamond content of the sludge, as you call it, although that could well contain a significant amount of stones. The mountain, or what is left of it, shows greater promise. It seems there is a strata containing the blue, as it is known, which would divulge diamonds, although there is no means of telling the size, or quality. It is significant enough to justify my Company initiating, mining operations. This of course would be expensive, it would be bringing in mining equipment, sieving, waxed sorting tables, individual visual sorters, etc. and security. This could turn out to be expensive, and would reduce the profit margin. If the yield was big enough…ok, but it often happens in the case of a small venture, as this appears to be the case, that it was hardly worth the major effort. However your initial suggestion, to the Assay Officer I believe, was to sell off claims. The responsibility to provide the means falls then to the claim owner. In my experience they would form a co-operative, and use one set of sorting for all. The proceeds would then be theirs, and we would only be involved from the point of view of our facilities being used, plus a security overview. My advice would be to pursue this line of thinking. Our findings would be available as support for the sale of claims, and the sale would be down to the Assay Office, save you from a major outlay." He smiled.

"Let's do it that way," said Brett, "Any other way is going to mean chaos around here and an invasion of our lives on the Ranch."

The others nodded.

"A wise decision." the Geologist said.

"How about the money from our diamond?" asked Janine.

"We would be happy to buy your diamond for £50,000 down payment, with a further payment of £35,000 after cutting and polishing has taken place, assuming our assessment is accurate."

"That's what's known as backing things both ways," remarked Brett, "You guys are on a win- win basis."

"The way it goes," said the geologist. "Best we can do folks."

"Better than a chunk of stone sitting on the bloody mantelpiece," remarked Cedric, "Thanks to Mariette."

They went to see the assay officer and outline the findings to him. He was delighted with their decision and pleased to have some significant business coming his way. The Geologist had already been to see him, and supply him with documents of authenticity and the assay officer was pleased to offer claims, to be purchased for $500 per half acre when, Cedric gave the ok.

Chapter 20

CHANCES

Craig decided that, with their share of the money he would invite Sir. John and, Lady Mary to visit the Ranch and enjoy a break in the world of down under. They were delighted with the news of the diamond find but also suggested an alternative. Apparently it was for their 50th Anniversary and in celebration they had been offered the facilities of the, *MISTRESS OF THE SEAS,* for a prolonged holiday. The owner was on a round the world cruise and would like the boat to be used, rather than stagnating in Singapore, where it was now docked and undergoing a refit. Their return would be to have the yacht sail to Singapore, and fly home from there. All their arrangements had been made and, Craig was averse to interfering, especially as the owner of the Mistress was pleased to have Singapore as the port to collect her for a sea voyage home. They were also looking forward to seeing their second grandchild who was due to arrive about the same time as they did. In the meantime they fenced off the proposed mining area with strict notices isolating it from the Ranch land, and gave the assayer the all clear to offer the claim sites for sale. At $1,000 an acre they stood to collect $500,000 less assay charges. Trade was brisk, as soon as the word got out men flocked to the office in Darwin. Men who were desperate to make money to offset their losses in the Cyclone, and those who were unable to ignore the fever attached to making a possible fortune. Within a week all claims had been sold, some sold again for many times their original price. There was however, an overlap from the fenced mining area extending half a kilometre on to the Ranch land. This was

Brett's idea on the basis that the force of the landslide could have pushed some diamonds to the farthermost extent. He felt it was worth investigating. He was proved later, to be right.

Anxious to follow the progress of Sir. John, Craig, phoned them and discussed their itinerary. He found Sir. John quite excited about the trip, especially as it would coincide with his 65th birthday and their anniversary. Reynard Manisty was to pick them up at Changi Airport in Singapore, and they would sail through the Malacca Strait and the Indonesian Islands to the Arafura Sea and on to Darwin. Manisty said there was no problem with the Modern day Pirates on this route, (which used to be a hotbed of Pirate activity) due to the co-operation between Indonesia and the Singapore Authorities. Piracy was, more or less, a thing of the past, unlike the East Coast of Africa where, Somalia spawned the worst attacks on shipping. On top of that a long time friend of Reynard, Captain Peter Stride R A N the skipper of HMAS, Geraldton, was to escort the Mai Maurau, a huge tanker on route to the far east, and suggested that the dates be coincided, so that protection could be afforded the Mistress of the Sea, at the same time. The Indonesia Navy also patrolled the Strait constantly. Craig was not at all happy, but as Sir. John, was so enthused he decided not to dampen his spirits and left it at that.

Meanwhile Janine was heavily pregnant and was being made a fuss of. She was older than she would have liked to be so far as childbirth was concerned, but enjoying good health, and high spirits, at the thought of seeing her parents again. The other good news was that Deborah, was engaged to be married having met a young Naval Lieutenant based in Portsmouth. She was over the moon, and according to Sir. John, he was a very dashing, and likeable young man with great prospects in the Royal Navy. Mariette was thrilled to bits.

Manado Bataan swore. Business was bad, too much interference from the Indonesian Navy and Singapore Authorities. There were rich pickings from piracy, about 40% of the worlds trade passes through the Straits, you'd think there would be plenty of opportunities to plunder; or better still reap a rich ransom. Not anymore. Bad enough that the bloody British Navy poked their nose in, but the Australian Navy took too much interest in what was none of their business. They would blow him out of the water, given half a chance, bloody Australians. He dare not fire back, too much risk. No point anyway. Even the trade ships had guns now, big guns some of them. Manado stood on Kelian Beach in Tanjung, such a good place to make successful raids. He lived on Banka Island, which formed the Eastern side of a narrow strip of sea lane, which was too narrow for these big ocean- going ships to manoeuvre or even out-run him. Now he was forced to stand and watch a fortune sail by. Mind you there were other ships. Rich yacht owners who were too scared of the African coast. Coast guards warned them off the Somalian coast, so they did venture into the Malacca Strait from time to time. Perhaps, he thought. His contacts had told him there would be a huge Chinese Tanker, the Mai Marau leaving Singapore quite soon, full of 50,000 tons of crude oil. Sure to have a naval escort, he thought bitterly. He went back to the village and the comfort of his wives. He had forgotten how many he had, somewhere around six, and as many daughters. All of them gave birth from time to time, and always had daughters. He did have two sons, now in their twenties from his first wife. He loved them dearly and was happy when he could give them gifts, or provide them with young Malaysian girls for the night. They were to take over when he decided to pack it all in, but he was fit, and very active and intended to keep hold of the reins for as long as possible. He would never let his sons take part in actual piracy though. They were too valuable to risk a stray bullet. They stayed at home and organized the ransom demands and the care of hostages, not that there were any at the moment!

The time passed quickly, the mining reaching frenetic pace stimulated by early finds of diamonds ranging from small industrial to medium size stones. One miner found a stone which was big enough to promise a multi-thousand value others unearthed smaller, but worthwhile diamonds. Brett organized a huge bulldozer which they used to shift the tail end of the sludge to well within the Ranch confines and arranged with the hands, for them to take turns in sifting through the huge mound on a fifty-fifty basis as long as they did not neglect their duties. It became a game of lucky dip, and bets were laid as to the first man to find a valuable stone.

Deborah was married to her sailor. She was radiant, and her husband Andrew Cunningham, proudly sporting a DFC on his immaculate number ones, was a popular addition to the family. They flew to the Maldives for two weeks, and, Sir. John and Mary, flew the next day to Singapore. Mary was entranced by the flight, never having flown before and they arrived on time at Changi, Airport.

Reynard himself was there to meet them and saw them settled in to the Yacht. They spent two days sightseeing in Singapore and set sail on a hot, and humid, sub tropical day in the wake of the Mai Marau, which loomed above them dwarfing the Mistress. They fell back avoiding the massive wake. There was no sign of HMAS Geraldon. Manisty concluded the destroyer would catch them up as they left the Singapore Strait. The sea breeze was a welcome relief. Sumatra loomed on the starboard side, and a multitude of small islands dotted the calm, and blue waters. Flying fish abounded, skimming the surface with silver wings, gliding effortlessly. Mary was unwilling to leave the upper deck, but was tempted below by the aromas issuing from the galley. As night fell the yacht dimmed all unnecessary lights, and Manisty, set a watch with strict instructions to be on the alert. There was a full moon and with the reflection off the water it was a bright, and entrancing night. At the same time Peter Stride, aboard the Geraldon, received an urgent message from C in C Pacific. His Yeoman stood by whilst, Peter, read the message.

HMAS Geraldon from C. in C. Pacific Most urgent. Survivors adrift 20 deg North…70 degrees East. Injured seamen. Urgent. Intercept ASAP. No other ship in vicinity."

"Shit!" Swore Stride. "Send a reply, Received Will go."

This took priority over all else. The Marau would have to go it alone.

"Bridge Charthouse," he called on the intercom.

"Charthouse?"

"We've got some bloody survivors floating about in the India Ocean, 20 degrees North 70 East, Give me a course Keith."

Keith Waterhouse, Navigating Officer, spread the chart open and rolled the rule across marking a red line. He did a cross reference and called the bridge back.

"We need to get out of Singapore reaches first, due North but the Pilot is aboard, then steer due West, that location is dead on the bloody Equator. I'll feed you the bearing as needed. How about the Maldives they're nearer than us?"

"As much as they can do to keep the bloody Islands afloat, let alone start rescue operations."

"Probably those fucking Somali's!"

"Have to delay the Marau."

"Too late she's under way, take miles for her to stop, and then she'd be blocking everyone else. They will have to slow down and wait for us to catch up. How long at full ahead?"

"Twelve hours, all going well. What about your mate on the Mistress?"

"Can't be helped, covering them was a personal favour really, nothing official. I'll inform them that we'll be late."

"You're right about that."

Manado Bataan stood on the huge rock at Remadong Beach a day or two later and peered through his binoculars. Dawn was just breaking with the suddenness of the Tropics, almost pitch dark one minute, and flooded with brilliant sun the next.

He peered into the Malacca Strait. Just fishing boats, no Tanker, "Ah well," he thought, "It's a long way to Singapore especially for a bloody great ship like that. What a prize though. They would be sure to pay a ransom; they would just have to stick the price up per barrel. Best to alert his men though, just in case, it would need all his resources, particularly as all ships carry firearms now. He clambered down off the rock, baggy trousers flapping in the early breeze, his face screwed up against the brilliant sun. He could feel that luck would be with him today, his eyes glittered with greed, he barred his blackened teeth in a grin and pushed his cap to the back of his head. He was a small man even by Malayan standards but with hardened muscles, and a spiteful temper. He ruled the village without pity, or sympathy. He passed the word around that all the men must stand by their small, but fast water crafts hidden in the many creeks and inlets around the island. All could swarm out of Keilian beach in a flash. In the good old days there had been ample practice, now it was too quiet. It all depended upon how big this damned tanker was. Too high in the water and scaling her side quickly would be a problem, possibility of men being killed, now that the Ships were allowed to defend themselves.

On board the Mistress, Reynard received a ship to ship radio message from the Geraldon.

"Need to rescue survivors. Official reassignment. Must take priority. Delayed, but will catch up ASAP. Stay with Marau just in case. Peter."

The same message went to the Captain of the Mai Marau. Sir. John told, Mary, of the change of circumstances and she became very worried.

"What if they attack us John, whatever will we do?"

"They won't bother with us, if they bother at all," said John, with more confidence than he felt. "There is a bigger prize in the Mai Marau. Whilst we are sheltered by her, we shall be ok. Besides piracy has been stamped out here. All the piracy happens off East Africa."

Mary was not convinced, especially as she saw, Reynard supervising the mounting, and preparing a Pom Pom gun on the foredeck. The gun was surplus stock after the war and he had bought it as an investment. It was brand new and had never been fired and had come with boxes of ammunition, including a tracer. She looked enviously at the huge tanker some half a mile ahead, and wished she was on board that, rather than the comparatively flimsy motor yacht.

Chapter 21

PIRACY

It was pitch black, Bataan was stood once more high on the rock. He peered into the blackness and saw nothing. 'Where the Hell was the tanker' It should have appeared by now, he waited for the dawn only half an hour away, fretting that the Navy would appear as well. As the first rays of the sun burst through the night he looked again. Still nothing, or was there? Something glinted in the morning light. He rubbed his eyes and looked again.

Yes, it was a ship; a huge ship, the sun reflected off the glass on the bridge, it was the Marau, still a mile away. Excited he blew on a cows horn which sent a mournful cry that could be heard by the waiting hordes. Bataan jumped up and down with joy. He peered again through the binoculars, no sign of the Navy. He cackled with delight. Along the coast, hidden in the thick undergrowth the waiting pirates prepared their boats, most were powerful crafts with outboard motors and inflatables. Others were strong canoes, fast when rowed by six men. All were armed with AK 47 rifles, as well as side-arms, most carried knives.

The captain of the Marau stood on the after bridge, they were approaching a tricky part of the strait where a ship of this size needed skilful handling to avoid running aground, or into the smaller islands scattered across the strait. He was also aware that Bangka Island was a favourite place for attacks on shipping. He had the crew stationed along the port side with rifles and axes and lookouts on the top of the Bridge. There was no sign that anything was amiss but he was angry that the, Geraldon, had, in his mind, deserted him. However, he shrugged; the rule of the sea was that saving human life was the top priority. As they drew nearer to Bangka Island a lookout shouted from the Port side of the bridge.

"Bridge-Lookout, Bandits ahead all spread out to surround us off the Port bow, hundreds of em."

Indeed there were hundreds of them, or so it seemed. The small boats sped across the still waters, their occupants screaming and firing rifles. The crew, conscious of the fact that they stood to lose their, Safe bonus if the ship was captured fought back. They carefully picked individuals and shot them dead. Some managed to get under the lee of the ship and sling grappling irons on to the deck which caught on the rails. As soon as they gripped, the pirates scrambled up the ropes like monkeys. Swift blows from an axe severed the ropes and sent the attackers tumbling back into the waters. It became obvious to Manado Bataan that they were getting nowhere with this onslaught, his men were getting shot, and the chances of overcoming the crew, who were well prepared, was remote. He called off the attack and watched, downhearted as the potential prize slid away from his grasp. Then he noted the, Mistress, which lay about 500 metres further up the strait. Manisty was endeavouring to turn the yacht around, desperate to avoid the hordes of bandits falling back from attacking the Marau. By doing so the Pom Pom was useless if fired, as they lay it would blow the bridge to smithereens. The hordes turned towards them and covered the distance in no time as the boat was broadside towards them. As the Pom Pom came to bare they opened fire. The shells spewed out of the eight barrels hitting very little, the crew unused to the gun, and panicking at the same time. The pirates surrounded the yacht on both sides and swarmed up the grappling ropes, the crew stood no chance. The helmsman was stunned by a blow from a rifle butt, and all were surrounded and threatened by a mad looking, bedraggled horde, brandishing AK 47's at them.

Reynard Manisty was distraught. Not only were they all at risk, but his multi-million pound yacht was at the mercy of a bunch of Heathen madmen Hell bent on mayhem, and destruction. He feared for Sir. John, and Lady Mary, how would they cope. He stood, tied with his hands behind his back, glowering at Manado, who smiled happily at the fuming Captain.

"Do you speak English, you bastard?" Manisty spat at him.

"I speak good English. I well educated. Welcome to Indonesia. I pleased to see you, with lovely ship, worth much money. You too rich man, pay plenty ransom."

"I am not a rich man, you'll get no ransom for me."

"Then you stay with me long time .Someone else pay ransom. Yes?"

"No," retorted Reynard.

"How about Lady, and Husband, they rich…high class… plenty money. They not like to stay long."

"None of us will stay long, the Coast Guard, and Navy will soon see to that. They will hang you by your scrawny neck and your thieving followers."

Manado laughed, "They have tried…we still here." His face changed from a smiling expression to one of anger. He barred his teeth. "Now you listen to me," he snarled. "You will stay here until money is paid, you," He waved his hand at the crew, "will not be hurt, if you behave, do as told, you go and get clothes and things."

He turned his back and waved to the man at the helm. The engines started and the Mistress slid smoothly away towards the Island. At least they can handle her, thought Manisty. The ship ran down the West side of Bangka Island and swung into what appeared, to be a thick area of undergrowth, which parted as the bows touched it, she passed through, and the bushes closed behind them. From seaward it seemed to have disappeared, they continued along the inlet and tied up at a makeshift jetty. They were invisible from sea, and from the air.

"They've done this before," thought the Captain ruefully.

Below in their cabin Sir. John, and Lady Mary, was held at gunpoint, Shocked at the onslaught that had taken place Mary hugged her dressing gown around her and glared at the two pirates who confronted her.

"You get dressed. You pack clothes. You do as told."

He shoved Mary and brandished the gun. Mary turned on him and slapped him across the face. Had it not been so serious John would have laughed. The expression on the face of the captor was one of utter shock, his eyes opened wide and his mouth gaped open. Women didn't dare to do such a thing, they were there to do what they were told, to be slapped by one was outrageous.

"Get out," said Mary, "Get out whilst I dress, you uncouth hoodlum."

Too shocked to do anything else, her captor turned and

left the cabin. The other, startled, followed him. They stayed outside the door.

John smiled, "That told em old girl, but it was a bit dangerous, he could have shot you."

Slowly they dressed and stuffed whatever clothing they could into a suitcase. They went up to the upper deck followed by the two pirates. Captain Manisty was there, his hands tied behind his back.

"So sorry about this, I thought we were safe, bloody navy never turned up, going to be hell to pay you'll see."

"You shut mouth. you no talk…I do talking." Manado shouted.

With that the crew, and the others, were shepherded off the boat, formed into a single line, and marched off into the jungle. Incredibly the accommodation was not as barren as they expected. All were herded into a long house, a raised timber dormitory with beds along each side. The place had obviously been previously occupied by earlier unfortunates; there was a wash house at one end with toilet facilities. None of it was clean, not to, Mary's standards and she was disturbed to think she was to share with all the men. However Manado, conscious that his captives were worth a huge ransom had one end partitioned off and made private for them.

"You can go walk-about, but there are guards around so you cannot escape. If you try you will be shot. Food will be brought two times a day. Good food…we must keep you well. Your boat will be untouched, that worth lots of money for me." He laughed his cackling laugh and left.

The honourable Percival Carstairs, Foreign Secretary,

studied the Vernons Football Coupon endeavouring to sort out those teams which would draw. He had no idea about any of the teams but tried to convince himself that he was due to win. There was a knock on the door and his under-secretary came in. Percival slid the coupon under his blotter.

"What?" He said irritably.

"Rather bad news I'm afraid Sir."

"Do you ever bring anything but! What is it this time trouble in Syria, or some other God forsaken place?"

"No Sir. Piracy in the Malacca Strait."

"Thought that had all stopped, all quietened down. Why these people have to go gallivanting about in countries they know nothing about I shall never understand. Which ship this time?"

"The Mari Maurau, very large tanker on its way to the Far east."

"That's Chinese isn't it; bugger all to do with us."

"It was attacked by pirates but managed to fight them off. Quite a gunfight, apparently."

"Good for them, so what's the bad news?"

"The pirates turned their attack on a private ocean- going yacht, British crew, owned by an ex Royal Naval Captain, sailed the yacht into one of the inlets and have taken the crew hostage. What is worse, Sir. is that two guests aboard the yacht are Sir. John Hadleigh, and Lady Mary Hadleigh, quite eminent people Sir."

"Well they should know better. I've heard of Hadleigh,

Merchant Banker isn't he?" Carstairs leaned back and scratched his thinning hair. "Who told them it was a safe area; those bloody Malaysians have been at it for years."

"With respect Sir. you did."

"Me!"

"Well this office Sir." Percival scowled.

"Have they been in touch; the pirates ask for a ransom or anything?"

"Not yet. The coast guard in Singapore needs to know the next of kin of the Hadleighs, we believe it to be their only daughter, a Mrs. Weston, she's in Australia, Darwin we think. That is being checked at the moment. She will have to be informed."

"Let me know of any developments. In the meantime send a strongly worded letter to these savages, via Singapore, to the effect that we demand the immediate release of all the hostages, and view their high handed actions to be criminal, and intolerable. Add something after the style of serious repercussions could result. Send the same memo to the Indonesian Authorities and ask them what the hell they are doing about it."

"Fat lot of good that'll do." Thought the under secretary and left.

Manado Bataan fiddled with the radio telephone and finally reached the Singapore Coast Guard.

"I have plenty hostages, valuable boat, two important people. They are safe and well and will be released for money. I want $ 1 million American Dollars for each. $1 million for boat,

$1 million for him, and $1 million for her. You understand? $3 million dollars plenty quick."

"Who's speaking?"

"I am chief of Bangka Island Pirates. You don't mess with me, you pay or else."

The Chief Coast Guard picked up the phone. "Listen to me you bloody savage, you let those people go. Piracy will not be tolerated and ransoms will not be paid. They do not have that sort of money and they wouldn't pay it if they had. Your only chance to avoid life long term imprisonment is to free them unharmed."

A Senior Officer signalled to the Coast Guard, and took the phone.

"Listen," he said calmly, "There is no need to get belligerent about this."

"What you mean belligerent?"

"Belligerent, losing tempers. We can work something out."

"Only thing need working out is $3 million dollars."

"These people haven't got that sort of money, it would have to come from their Government and that takes time to arrange."

"I don't care where it comes from, as long as it comes."

"We need time. Time to contact the right people, time to contact the family; it will be weeks if not longer. I will do all I can to arrange for this but I need time. If they come to any harm, or ill treatment, the deal is off."

"You agree then, you agree to pay."

"I'll do my best; give me a number where I can reach you."

"Ok, ok I give you number, you ring me, you have two weeks." Manado was jubilant, "They going to pay $3 million dollars, we rich again."

He danced around his baggy trousers flapping. The information was passed to the Police in Darwin who knew the whereabouts of Janine. The Duty Officer drove to the Ranch and broke the news to them all. Janine burst into tears and clung to Cedric.

"Mummy won't stand up to this sort of treatment, and nor will Daddy, it will be the death of them. To think of them amongst all those creatures is terrible. What can we do? Do the authorities in the UK know about this, what are they doing?"

The Officer nodded. "The UK Foreign Secretary, Singapore Coast Guard and the Indonesian Coast Guard are all aware of what has happened. They all express their sorrow ma'am."

"I don't want their sorrow; they must get my parents out of there, before they suffer how the hell did this happen? My Husband spoke to the Captain of the Yacht and he assured us that there was no risk, not any more; the damned Foreign office confirmed this. They are responsible, send the Navy in or something." She sobbed into Cedric's shoulder.

Cedric nodded at the Officer. "Thanks for letting us know, keep us informed of everything that transpires."

"Of course Sir." he said and then as an afterthought, "They are demanding $3 million American dollars as a ransom."

"Jesus Christ!" blasphemed Brett, "who do they think we are?"

"I'm afraid it is Sir. Johns, title which gives them the impression of wealth." He smiled and left. After a while Janine, composed herself and sat unhappily in the lounge.

"Perhaps the Foreign Office will do something," she said hopefully, "or the Singapore Police."

"I wouldn't hold your breath," said Brett. "They haven't done much of a job in the past. The last time there were people released it took twelve months plus. I have an idea though." Janine looked up.

"I know a man."

Cedric laughed, "Brett you always know a man," Brett ignored him. "He could be expensive, but he could be the answer. Leave it with me at the moment. He went to his room and pulled a battered address book out of his case. He poured himself a scotch from a bottle on the side table, lit a cigarette and dialled a number on his cell phone.

Chapter 22

AMENDS

The phone rang and a husky female voice answered.

"I'd know that sexy voice anywhere," said Brett, "What colour is your underwear today?"

"That can only be one person, *Brett Carrington*, which unfortunate girl's bed did you crawl out of today?"

"Not unfortunate, she was delighted. They are always delighted, remember Surfers Paradise?"

"What do you want Brett?" Jane ignored the barb, but her mind flicked back.

"Seriously, Jane, I am a reformed character." A snort on the phone.

"I am now a wealthy Cattle Ranch partner in Darwin, leading a wholesome life."

"Yeah right! Where have you been? It's been ages?"

"Seriously, I need to talk with Tug, it's important."

"Well he's not here; I can give you a phone number. Over, or below the Radar?"

"Definitely below." She gave him a number.

"Thank you my love, I shall see you soon."

"No rush… no rush at all," she said sarcastically.

"You can really hurt a man, but you're wonderful." Brett broke the connection and dialled again.

"Yeah…"

"Tug, you bloody reprobate, where are you?"

"Is that you Brett, really you? Where the hell have you been buddy? I haven't seen or heard from you in ages. I'm in Singapore, having a break from the wicked world."

"You bloody beauty, I bet I know where in Singapore, propped up in the bar at Raffles with a large Chivas Regal."

"Nearly right, it's Famous Grouse, they need to upgrade here. How can I help?"

"Serious situation Tug, need to talk face to face, can't speak over the phone."

"Where are you Brett?"

"Darwin."

"Shit, can you get to Jakarta?"

"No problem, when?"

"Tomorrow I can meet you at the Airport, Jakarta Main Airport .Phone me with the ETA."

Brett disconnected. Another phone call and he was booked on a direct flight the next morning at 6 am. As Brett got off the plane he spotted Tug Cartwright immediately. A big man, 6ft.2ins, with shoulders too wide to pass through a door comfortably. He was dressed in khaki shirt and shorts with desert boots, matching deeply tanned legs. His battered cowboy hat sweat stained was tilted to the back of his head, a shock of light brown hair tumbling around his shoulders. He was chatting to an official airside, and smoking a cigarette. He spotted, Brett, and strode across the tarmac.

"Hello you reprobate, welcome to the den of iniquity."

He shook Brett's hand with a fist full of huge fingers and grinned with obvious pleasure.

"Come on," he said, "transport over here, no need for customs and all that crap, thank Christ for corruption."

Brett wondered how he managed to get airside, now he knew. They drove out of the airport and took the main road to Bandung, but turned off quite soon at Bekasi towards Batujaya, chatting about past escapades. Tug had been a Marine Commando for ten years. Established him as a formidable character and achieved the rank of, Colonel before resigning, and setting up a Mercenary force. "More dollars in this life," he would say. He met Brett, in Hong Kong years before, at a poker game in the back streets. He admired Brett's skill, knew he was cheating, but couldn't work out how. They formed a friendship and had some wild times together. Brett had been to his office before in a building on the outskirts of a private aerodrome in Batujaya, it was an insignificant location and gave cover for two ex-helicopter gunships obtained by devious means. After an hour they arrived and parked the silver and black Range Rover at the rear of the building. Apart from one light aircraft taxiing to take off, there was no-one about. Upstairs they went into the office through a door marked, Cartwright Enterprises.

"That told no-one anything," grinned Brett. The office was bathed in sunlight and was exceptionally tidy and professional. Jane sat at a computer and looked up as they entered. Brett walked straight over and planted a kiss full on her lips.

"God I've missed you," he said.

"Liar," Jane, was flustered, she coloured up, "you're mad."

"Put that girl down," said Tug, "You don't know where she's been."

Tug ushered Brett through into an inner office. A huge cluttered desk faced the window, there were two settees and some chairs and a drinks cabinet.

"Can we have some coffee please Jane, lots of it."

"I'll put some bromide in his."

Tug shrugged, "There you go Brett, a woman scorned and all that. Now tell me, tell me all of it from the beginning."

They talked, smoked, and drank coffee and talked some more. Brett told him of the past years, of the Weston's, the Ranch, the diamond find and distress at the kidnapping. Occasionally, Tug, would ask a question but he listened and thought. Later Tug poured a couple of hefty whiskies, looked at some notes he had made and walked across to the window. He could see the ocean from there. He was quiet, thinking.

"Bangka Island you say? That rings a bell, that rings a loud bell. Drink up we're off to Prison."

Chapter 23

FEAR

The prison on the outskirts of Jakarta was a grim looking building. Barbed wire topped the walls, and the doors were huge and solid. They parked and Tug, rang the bell. A guard dressed in a ragged uniform opened the door. Tug spoke in fluent Malay; the man looked suspiciously at them, but relaxed after a handful of money quickly disappeared into his pocket. They walked behind the guard; the place stunk of unwashed humanity and stale food. He took them to a cell at the far end and opened the door, closing it with a clang behind him. Inside was an Asian man dressed in ragged clothes, hair unkempt and filthy. He was about 30 years old, thought Brett. His eyes were sunk back but glittered as he looked at Tug. He was sat on a chair at a stained table bolted to the floor.

"I shall need to take this man for interrogation, have I permission to do this?" Tug asked the guard.

The guard fingered the wad of notes in his pocket. He nodded, "He is of no importance to us, and he does not exist. He is just a filthy terrorist."

Tug nodded, noting the puzzlement in the man's eyes. "First I must ask him some questions, perhaps you would leave us."

The guard nodded again and left the cell, locking the door behind him. Bret, walked over to the corner of the cell and crossed his legs, leaning on the wall.

"Your name is Asif Mohammed. Your are a Moslem, one of the bad Moslems, a terrorist?" Said Tug. He walked casually around the table and suddenly kicked the chair from under, Asif who sprawled in a heap on the floor.

"I am not a terrorist; I was a Pirate, nothing more. I have done no harm." He picked himself up and stood by the table. "Who are you? What do you want with me?"

"Who I am doesn't matter, what I am, Is different. I am a man who always means what he says, always does what he promises, and doesn't give a fuck for the consequences. Understand?" The man said nothing. "I bring good news...bad news, and even worse news. Also three choices for you. What you tell us will determine which of the choices you decide to accept."

Asif still said nothing but an arrogant sneer crossed his face.

"First the good news...You will be taken from here, and flown by helicopter to Bangka Island, where you will be set free, no longer a prisoner. That is if you tell us what we need to know, truthfully, no lies, no bullshit." Asif frowned, puzzled. "Now the bad news. If you do not give us the information you will still be taken from here and hung by cable below a helicopter and dropped in the Flores Sea, in a bay, known as "Shark Bay," where the Tiger shark and the Great White gather. Do you know the place? There was silence. "We will dangle you a few feet above the water. Have you ever seen a Great White leap for his prey, incredible, they leap five or more feet? They would get your legs first. Then we pull you up, still almost alive and stitch you in a wild pigs skin and bury you to suffocate in the stench of wild pig."

"You would not dare to do such a thing, you bullshit me."

Tug looked him straight in the eyes. Quietly he said. "Nothing would give me greater pleasure Asif. I have seen what terrorists like you do to innocent children and people, and I have waited to get this chance. I always do what I say remember? Remember, I'll fuck you up on this earth, and fuck your chances of Paradise."

Up to that point the sneer still stayed on the face of Asif, but the threat of the pigskin broke him. He broke down, his eyes brimmed with tears and he shook with terror. There was no doubting this bloody man would do as he said.

"Please, I tell you anything, everything I can. I am a good man, I have wife and three children, not seen them for two years. I am a good man please don't do this terrible thing."

Brett had turned pale.

"Right "said Tug. "Manado Bataan, he is the leader of the pirates. Right?" Asif nodded. "Tell me about him."

"He is a cruel man, very rich; he doesn't harm prisoners because they mean money to him. He lives in Village with his women and daughters, his sons live north of the village separately. He greatly loves his sons, they are from his first wife, who he loved...she died from Malaria. His wives only bear him daughters; he has no time for daughters. His sons are not allowed to be pirates in case they get killed; they live in luxury with different women each night. They get everything; men who take risks get next to nothing." He spat on the floor.

"You say they live north of the village, anywhere near the huge rock at Remadong?"

Asif looked surprised, "How you know that?"

"Never mind, do they?"

"Yes only 100 metres away, big house, plenty of guards, guard dogs, wire fence. Why you want to know this?"

Tug ignored him. "What else?"

They drunk, most nights, sometimes they bring virgins from the village and rape them. Manado say, and do nothing."

"Nice people!"

"When they attack the shipping do they gather at Kelian beach?"

"All down that coast, mainly Kelian Beach, some hide in the river mouth, they all join in the attack. They keep fuel near the beach for the boats. I don't know nothing else Sir. I would tell you, I don't tell any lies, all I say is true. Please, please." He wept.

Tug looked at Brett, who glanced at the poor wretch. "I think we can believe him."

Tug nodded.

"All right Asif, if what you say is true you have nothing to worry about, we will set you free later, unharmed, with perhaps some money as well. I promise, and as I say, I always keep my promises."

The relief on Asif's face was immense, he still sobbed but he smiled. "Thank you Sir. thank you."

"Yeah right," said Tug.

They left, and Tug spoke to the guard again. "No harm comes to him, you understand? You feed him properly, you treat him properly, we will be back soon to collect him. There will be plenty more American dollars for you. Clear?"

The Guards face lit up, more money .he nodded. "Certainly I guard him with my life."

"It might come to that," muttered Tug.

"You'd better stay over tonight Brett, there is only one hotel, quite decent, Jane has set up a permanent residence there. Right next to a Chinese Restaurant that serves a decent meal. I'll book you a room."

Tug dialled a number. "Now let's have a proper meal. All of us, I can pick you up in the morning. Both of you and take you to the Airport."

They enjoyed a full spread of Chinese delicacies and a couple of bottles of wine until quite late, then Tug took his leave.

As they waved him off Brett said, "Drink?"

Jane nodded, "Why not."

There was an orchestra playing soft music in the bar. They each had a highball and danced a bit talking over times gone by. Ultimately they went to their rooms and said a reserved goodnight. A little later, Brett looked out of his room along the corridor, Jane's door was ajar. He crept along and pushed it open, went in and closed it after him. The next morning Tug picked them up. Jane sat in the front with Tug.

"Both sleep well?" said Tug cheerily, glancing out of the corner of his eye at Jane, who looked particularly beautiful. "Did you put any Bromide in his coffee?"

"We've run out."

"That's a good job then."

Jane coloured up, "You just watch the road."

Tug settled down in his office. A plan was forming in his mind. He dialled a number.

"Singapore traffic. Bill Mcintyre please, Tug Cartwright here."

Bill Mcintyre was head of the sea going traffic entering, and leaving Singapore. He and his parents had been trapped in Singapore when it was invaded by the Japanese during the War. He, as a young lad was bundled on to the last ship to leave, which was the last time he ever saw them. After the War, as a youth he returned to Singapore to find out what had happened to them. He could find no trace. Rather than desert them again he had remained in Singapore and was now in charge of the shipping using the port. He was a broad Scot and had never lost his accent. He came on the phone.

"Well, as I live and breathe, how are you Tug?" The rolling Scottish brogue was unmistakable. "There is something I can do for you, there always is!"

They chatted for a few minutes, "Bill I need to know the shipping movements down the Malacca Strait for the next week or 10 days. Type and size of ship. Time of sailing destination and nationality. Can do?"

"Reckon so, anything to do with those heathen pirates Tug?"

"In a way, could you fax them to me." He gave his fax number. "I would be very grateful. Be a couple of Drams in it for you."

"On top of those you promised last time."

"That's why a Scot is related to the bloody elephant…never forgets."

He then asked Jane to send e'mails to the members of his team. "To all chickens, gather round mother Hen. PDQ."

On the drive to the Airport, Brett asked, "Any place for me in whatever you have in mind?"

Tug smiled, "I don't think so Brett. There is no-one I would rather have by my side in a free- for- all ruckus in a Bar. But what I have in mind is not your scene. You felt sorry for that little bastard in the Jail, when he blubbered." He looked at Brett.

Brett nodded, "He seemed genuine, you wouldn't have done those things you threatened, would you? You put the shits up me, let alone him."

"Trust me I would…that was all an act, put Laurence Olivier to shame they would. Underneath he is still a twisted evil little swine who would strap a pound of Semtex to his arse and blow up as many people up as he could. But I'm pretty sure he told the truth. Any one of my guys would slit the enemy's throat, or break his neck without breaking step. Would you?"

"No, I couldn't."

"Exactly, you're too nice a guy, that's why I won't involve you. Hesitate and you could lose your life, and we don't want that do we? You go home Brett, and console the family. Tell them to do nothing, not speak to anyone and to carry on as best they can. Leave it to me, and within a week or ten days they will all be sailing free."

They said their goodbyes at the airport and, Brett, watched

Tug, drive off. He went to the Departure lounge and waited
for his flight.

Chapter 24

THE PLAN

Jane walked in amongst them. "All coming, except one, Cliff."

"What's up with him?" asked Tug.

"He's in prison."

"What."

"He's got 30 days for assault. Beat up the husband who found him in bed with his Wife." She grinned, "If you lot used your brains as much as you do your genitals you'd be a brilliant lot." She wiggled her bottom as she walked out.

"You're just jealous Jane." She raised one finger.

Tug rang Bill Mcintyre. "Any changes Bill, thanks for the Fax."

"Only one. The Geralton got back, Came in like a rat with its arse on fire, managed to save the lives of 10 British seaman though. Been reallocated to shadow the S. S. Capetown, a Merchant ship bound for South Africa, going through the Malacca strait."

"What date?"

"The 27th slips anchor at 6 pm."

"Thanks Bill." Tug turned his attention to the charts spread on his desk. Beauty, you bloody beauty. Right lads tomorrow morning 6 am here. Get a good night's sleep. No trouble. Capiche!"

They all gathered at 6 am including those who had come later and set to work planning the attack. Tug told them the basic background, and of the information obtained from Asif. "We fight fire with fire," he said. "Manado kidnaps our lot so we kidnap his two sons. We cannot hope to get the hostages out, there are too many, but having his sons in our clutches gives us the edge. These bastards are all terrorists at heart, so no quarter given. No guns unless we get trapped, knives and throttling best weapons. One shot and the whole place will be on us. We go in by sea and land here." He prodded the map just east of the huge rock at Remadong. "There is a small inlet with a beach there. The Village is here, and the sons live here. We should come to their houses first, not have to avoid the village. Time is of the essence the chopper will swoop in, land, pick us up and be away like a dose of salts. There will only be two minutes at most so we must be in position just before dawn, 5.30 am. Take off before daylight, these guys have rocket launchers. We go at dusk on the 29th. By that time the S.S. Cape town will be viewable from Bangka Island, shadowed by H.M.A.S Geraldon. That should put a stop to any attempt to board the Cape Town, but the whole bloody band of Pirates will be gathered on, and around Kelian Beach, keeping them away from where we are. Any questions so far?"

Carl Bruno a German, ex-legionnaire, lounged on the settee smoking a vile smelling cigar. He was six footer, like the others and weighed 280 lbs. Belying his appearance he was a genial and easy going man, who rarely lost his temper. His sheer strength had been the saviour of most of the team at one time.

"Are we swimming in, or in the inflatable's Tug?"

"Only six of us will actually carry out the raid. We'll use an inflatable, mainly to keep the firearms dry, have to ditch it afterwards. I want three in the chopper and one or two keeping an eye on Keiling beach, to keep us informed of what the bastards get up to. Those two can beach with the others and then make their way through these paths to be in place as we locate the target. We shall all have two way intercom contact, there are sentries and a barbed wire fencing, plus guard dogs. Those are no problem; some steak laced with chloramphenicol will put them out. We need them to find the meat before they find us. If that's all, there is nothing to do but wait and hope that things stay as they are. Further briefing nearer the time."

The meeting broke up. All preparations had been made by the 27th. H.M.A.S Geraldton had sailed a mile astern of the S S Cape Town, which was travelling at a steady 9 knots. The team had gone over the attack in detail and all was checked again. They would set off at dusk on the 29th flying into the ocean north of Remadong, at least a mile away from the coast, and travel by inflatable boat to the beach. It was to be the beach where they would be picked up at 5 am prompt the next morning. The time was imperative, if they arrived any later, there was a risk the chopper would be spotted, any earlier and the risk was the same. The landing went well, they boat coasted into the beach in pitch darkness, they hauled it into the undergrowth and moved carefully along the route to where they hoped the two sons of Manado, were asleep in a drunken stupor. Wearing assault clothing and infra red lamps they trod carefully and broke out of the undergrowth quite suddenly. A barbed wire fence confronted them. Quietly they snipped a hole and checked for booby traps. They stopped and listened. A movement to their left alerted Tug. He held up his hand and all froze. A sentry was stretching and yawning almost on top of them. Tug gestured to one of the team, who slid through the gap silently creeping up behind the man, he grabbed him around the throat, turned his head to the left and sharply to the right, breaking his neck. He lay the body down and gestured to the others, they slid through the gap. There was a sudden puzzled bark, they all sank to the ground, one of the guard dogs appeared snuffling around suspiciously. Tug threw a handful of doctored steak towards it. It gobbled up a chunk and sniffed around for more. Two other dogs appeared and there was a scuffle as they scented the meat and grabbed what they could. Another handful was thrown and wolfed down. They waited, silent and hidden in the darkness. It took only ten minutes for the drug to take effect and the dogs collapsed and twitched unconscious. The team moved across the field and suddenly the house, appeared in the early mist. Tug stopped and signalled. He smelled tobacco. Another sentry was sat against the side of the long--house smoking. Tug moved around in a circle and one swift movement buried his knife in the mans heart, clamping his other hand across the mans mouth. He died without making a sound. There appeared to be no efforts to guard the inhabitants of the house and they moved in, the door creaked and there was a fly screen of beads within. An oil lamp lit the interior dimly. There were two beds, one on each side, the place stunk like a brewery and the snores of the two men, was deafening in the silence. Each bed had a naked woman curled up alongside the men, and two other women were asleep at the far end of the house, on blankets.

Two of the team went to each bed, the woman was rolled off on to the dirt floor and woken, startled faced with the muzzle of an AK 47 pointed at her face and the terrifying sight of a masked man holding it. They didn't need telling to be quiet. The other members of the team pressed a chloroform soaked pad across the mouths of the sleeping bandits. They struggled but succumbed very quickly. They were bundled into heavy plastic body bags and zipped up. Tug herded the two women to the far end, waking the others and spoke quietly Malay.

"If you make one sound, if you move, I will kill you all. You stay here and not go to the village…You understand?"

They huddled together, terrified. Tug followed the team, two men each carrying the sons of Manado, and went swiftly across the field and into the jungle. The dogs still slept.

Chapter 25

TAKEN

Manado was settled in his usual position on the top of the rock, watching for the Cape Town, It should be along soon he hoped. In the distance he heard the sound of a helicopter, the unmistakable clatter of the rotors. He frowned; the sound grew louder, and then went quiet. Within minutes it came again, and then died slowly away. 'Bloody Indonesian Coastguards' he thought, 'Always snooping about can't leave anyone in peace. He settled back again to his watch. It was a further half an hour before he saw the lights of the Merchant Ship. First a white mast head light, then the red port light gleamed. The shape of the ship materialized out of the darkness. He blew frantically on his horn. Along the coast the pirates came to life from their hiding places and boarded their boats, manoeuvring out into the deeper water. Tugs' lookouts, spotted the movement amongst the undergrowth and reported to Tug.

"On the move Tug, dozens of them too far to see much, but heard the horn blow. You should be in the clear."

On board the Cape Town, the lookouts had also spotted the threat from the boat loads of villainous looking men bearing down on them. They lined the upper deck with modern weapons, and started firing as soon as the marauders were within range. They were also armed with grenades which were thrown amongst the craft and exploded like depth charges with enough power to capsize the boats. Manado had clambered down from his perch and got to the beach in time to see the carnage taking place. Suddenly there was a shriek in the air and a massive explosion amongst those still on the beach. Next came the Crump, from the still dark waters astern of the ship. Startled, Manado, saw the Geraldton appear, 4.5 inch guns trained and a further shell burst not too far from him. Terrified he screamed at his men to abandon the attack and they scattered in panic back to the beach.

Still the Geraldton fired. Four more shells ravaged the beach. Manado was out of his mind, he had expected time to get aboard the Cape Town, not caught with his trousers down a second time. Tears of anger flooded down his cheeks. He scuttled into the woods only to be met by one of the women from the Village. She had braved escaping from the long house and rushed to tell Manado, of the kidnapping. Terrified she blurted out a garbled version of what had happened. He slapped her face and snarled.

"Quiet, tell me so I understand what you mean, my sons gone, how they gone?"

She managed to compose herself and ran with him as they went to the Village. Manado raced into the house. The women were still huddled in the corner, wailing. He saw the beds, empty and upturned and he went berserk. One woman stood and went to speak, but he shot her dead.

"Why you no stop them?" he screamed. "Useless, useless bloody harlots."

Gathering a group of men he raced across the field in pursuit of the kidnappers. He found the dogs, still unconscious and shot them. Further on, the sentry lay crumpled against a tree, dead. Manado shot him again for good measure, in his madness. Tug, with his team reached the rendezvous, with minutes to spare. The still unconscious sons were dumped on the ground, to the relief of the men who had carried them. They sank to the ground and listened. They had heard the boom of the guns from the Geraldton, when a mile away from their pickup point and estimated they would just about make the deadline. There was no sign of the helicopter. A sudden crashing in the undergrowth alerted them, and two men appeared. The lookouts had made a beeline for the pickup point as soon as the attack by the Pirates fizzled out.

"You nearly got half a dozen bullets up your arse," laughed Tug.

His men safe they caught the clatter of the helicopter. It swept in from the sea and settled like a Dragonfly on the skimpy beach. Within a minute the two captives had been unceremoniously bundled in and the team clambered in behind them just as the pirates, led by Manado, burst out of the forest. Two of the pirates opened fire until Manado, jumping about like a ruptured frog screamed, "Don't shoot. my sons... my sons are in there!"

They stood, helpless, watching as the helicopter swept away out to sea.

Chapter 26

DIAMONDS

Those back on the Ranch were at a loss, worried as to what was taking place, they tried to find activities which kept their minds off the fate of the hostages. Brett ambled across where some of the Ranch hands were trying their luck at sifting through the still, considerable mound of dried sludge. He moved towards a mound a distance away, and picked up a pick and shovel. Stripping off his shirt he set about breaking the mound down into manageable heaps. It was hard work in the relentless sun, but he persevered. He straightened up and mopped the sweat off his forehead. A glint of blue caught his eye uncovered by his digging. He walked over and kicked at it. He thought he had broken his toe, the 'blue' turned out to be solid rock, a chunk of mineral, a strata of light blue running through it. Intrigued he brought down the point of the pick. The surrounding rock disintegrated but the blue, was still intact. Again he slammed at the blue and his pick rang like a tapped wineglass but it came away from the encasing rock. He levered it away and examined it. Opaque with streaks of gravel inside. He hit it again with the pick. Nothing, he stood up and looked at it. Suddenly it fractured by itself, literally falling apart. He was unaware of Mariette, who had walked over to see what he was up to until he heard her gasp.

"Do you know what this is Brett?"

"Oh hi Mariette, thought I would play about and see what was what."

"That is a chunk of what they call the blue Brett. It invariably contains diamonds, in the past prospectors have ignored it, too hard to break into, but exposure to the weather, and sunlight, weakens it and it does exactly what it's done, falls apart."

Brett looked at the heap of blue stone and grinned. "Do you reckon there's diamonds there then?"

"Let's have a look."

Mariette dragged one of the sieves across from a nearby pile and, Brett shovelled the blue chunks into it. Between them they shook the sieve, as they did so the blue stone broke up even more. Tiny sparkles of light glittered amongst the dust. Mariette picked one up, then another. Although they were small, they were, without doubt diamonds. Both excited they scrabbled through the gravelly mixture, and unearthed about a dozen more. Brett casually chucked aside a lump of blue the size of an apple which the fell apart. Mariette squealed, inside was a rough diamond, almost as large as the mantelpiece monster as they had christened the original find.

"It's a beauty Brett," she said, "a real beauty. You've hit the Jackpot." They hugged each other like two excited children.

"We have," said Brett, "I would have just sworn at the stuff for nearly breaking my toe."

They hurried back to break the news to the others.

"There could be more there you know." said Mariette.

"Let's leave them for the lads to find."

Tug picked up the phone and dialled Bill Mcintyre. "Bill, do you have a number where I can reach this little swine on Bangka Island. He got in touch demanding cash I believe?"

"Hello Tug, Yes he has some sort of radio telephone, he's sitting there waiting for news of the cash…any luck so far?"

"All going to plan so far Bill." Bill gave him the number. The phone rang; there was very little delay before Manado answered.

"Listen to me you bastard," said Tug. "We have your sons in custody; so far they are safe and unharmed. If you ever want to see them again you will do exactly what I tell you. Do you understand?"

"Why you no pay money?" Manado whined.

"You'll get no money, you're lucky to be alive. Now listen, you will put all the hostages and crew back on their boat with food and water. Unharmed, you hear me, unharmed. They will be allowed to leave at Dawn on Friday 31st."

"I kill them all if you no pay money!"

"Up to you, if you hurt any of them I shall dangle you sons under a helicopter and take them to Shark Bay, There I will drop them into the mouths of the Tigers and Great whites, a nice unexpected lunch."

"Aaah Eeeh, you filthy murderer, you would not dare to do that."

"Believe me, I will, and I will enjoy seeing them torn to pieces, now shut up. On top of that, the Destroyer HMAS Geraldton will be ready to take them safely on their journey. Any attempt to interfere, and the Geraldton, will lay off and blow your village and everyone in it to hell. Clear?"

Manado gave in. "Ok, ok. I do what you want, you not hurt my sons, and you set them free."

Tug disconnected. Tug then made a ship to shore call to the Geraldton and spoke to Peter Stride. He told him the arrangement and asked if the ship could be in the vicinity of Bangka Island at dawn on the 31st, just to show the flag and to undertake safe conduct for the yacht.

"It means leaving the Cape Town to her own devices," said Stride doubtfully. "On the other hand I suppose what you ask comes under the heading of protecting lives. I shall have to turn about and make speed to be there, but I guess it can be done."

Tug thanked him. He said nothing about blasting the village to pieces, knowing Peter Stride, would never agree to do that, but Manado didn't. As Dawn broke over the Strait the hostages were all led to the jetty and boarded the Mistress, food and water was also loaded. Manado did nothing but watch sullenly. His dreams of wealth evaporating before his eyes. The Gods were cruel he decided. Surely they could smile on him once in a while. He fretted about his sons, would they be freed. Whoever this man was, he sounded as though he could be trusted, but you never know. The thought of his sons being torn to pieces by sharks made him shudder.

"Ah! Well, there would be other ships." He shouted at the hostages to get a move on. Now it was happening he wanted to be done with it. Suddenly the sound of a helicopter broke the silence of the dawn, and from around the headland a Gunship appeared. Hanging beneath it were two bodies, roped together, wriggling with fright. Manado clapped his binoculars to his eyes. The Chopper was only 50 feet from the ground; the bodies were easily recognizable as his sons. Manado shrieked and pranced about in a panic. The gunship swung around and hovered above the yacht, watching as she sailed slowly away. At the end of the waterway it turned south and gathered speed.

Tug grabbed a loudhailer and yelled, "Are you all ok, anyone hurt?"

Captain Manisty, who couldn't believe his eyes at what had happened waved and stuck up two thumbs, the crew also waved and danced about on the deck. The helicopter then turned and swooped low over the village, the bodies, swinging like the pendulum of a huge clock, and bore away swiftly out of sight. Manado's two sons, almost unconscious, and feeling violently sick, were dumped at the extreme end of the Island. As the yacht sailed away, the Geraldton came into view, the Captain spoke to Reynard Manisty.

"Suggest you come aboard and leave a skeleton crew on your boat. We will take you in tow and proceed to Darwin. Welcome Home."

"Tug turned and grinned at his team, "Well done lads. I love it when a plan comes together."

Chapter 27

REUNITED

The news of the rescue soon reached Darwin, and the Chief of Police rang Cedric. Having had no news at all for many days they were ecstatic. The estimated time of the arrival of HMAS Geraldton was noon on the 3rd and preparations were made for a jubilant welcome, not only at the Ranch, but at the Port in Darwin. Coupled with the find of another very significant diamond, it seemed that ten Christmases had all come at once. Brett was the hero of the hour and, although he had said nothing about the rescue plans up to then, he now told them what had been arranged. He still didn't know the finer details. His attempt to put the cash from his diamond find into the general kitty fell on deaf ears.

"Won't hear of it, Brett you found it, it is yours."

"But Mariette found it with me; I'd have chucked it away without her."

Mariette smiled, "no way, you put it in your hip pocket Brett, after what you have done you deserve it."

"Take her out for a night on the town," piped up Janine, secretly watching Craig's face.

"Not bloody likely," Craig glowered, "I'll nail her shoes to the floor first."

Brett grinned, "Worth a try, anyway Tug will want paying for his expenses at least, leave that to me."

Tug related the details of the rescue to Brett, when asked how much the exercise cost he laughed.

"Be my guest Brett, you can buy the team a beer next time we meet."

"Rubbish" said, Brett, "there were helicopter costs, money for the team, apart from your time and expertise."

"Wonderful experience for the lads, and a wonderful result, forget it Brett. Come and see us soon, Jane misses you," he added slyly.

Brett put his diamond in a small birds nest on the mantelpiece, "There it will stay until any of us need the money, my lucky talisman."

The celebration on arrival of the Geraldton with the Mistress in tow seemed to involve the whole of Darwin. The local band turned out and played the National Anthem much to the delight of Peter Stride, and the crew. It was ages before they got back to the Ranch and sat down to a special meal, courtesy of Ho Chin.

"Cheer up Mary," said Sir. John, noting a worried expression on her face," have another glass of wine."

"I'm all right," said Mary, "but I left my best hat behind."

Janine nearly choked, Sir. John, sat open mouthed until all burst out laughing, then Mary saw the funny side too, and laughed with them. She, and Sir. John, stayed for a few months and saw the devastation of Darwin. They marvelled at the speed, and efficiency of the clear up operation, Darwin was already growing into the magnificent City it is today. They then flew home via Singapore.

Epilogue

2 YEARS LATER

Cedric, and Janine, stood in the Graveyard of Hadleigh Church holding hands and looking at the two graves. Mary due mainly to the deterioration in her health from her bad experience, had contracted double pneumonia and passed away in her sleep nearly 12 months before. Sir. John heartbroken, and completely at a loss, died some 6 months later. From a broken heart the Doctor said. Hadleigh Hall, he had bequeathed in its entirety to Janine, and Craig, together with a huge sum of money and the Death Duties (Now Inheritance Tax) had been paid by an Insurance policy taken out for just that exigency. Janine dried a tear.

"They were such lovely people, and such marvellous parents." She fingered the locket given to her years before.

Her latest offspring, three year old Mary, came skipping up and held Janine's hand.

"Are you crying mummy? Are you sad because Grandma, and Grandpa, has gone to Heaven?"

"Yes darling."

"Should I cry too?"

"No, they always saw you happy, smiling and laughing. I shall put a fresh flower on their grave every day, and I shall smile."

Mary ran off just as silver Mercedes pulled up and the back door spewed out Deborah, and her two children. They all walked slowly toward the Church for the In Memoriam Service.

"I found my old Triumph motor bike in the garage," Cedric said, "I might do it up, drive around the lanes looking for a young blonde mad driver."

"You'd better not, besides you're the Squire of the Manor now. Have to shoot pheasants and wear plus fours. They smiled.

"Yeah Right! said, Cedric…

Cyclone